LIMINAL SPACE

LIMINAL SPACE

VICKI-ANN BUSH

ALSO BY VICKI-ANN BUSH

Alex McKenna & The Geranium Deaths

Alex McKenna & The Academy of Souls – Audible Edition

Alex McKenna & A Winter's Night - Audible Edition

UNTHREADED

Ophelia

The Garden of Two

Saving A Life

The Queen of IT

Winslow Willow the Woodland Fairy

The Darkest Light

Short Stories

The Joshua Tree

Published in the United States by Creative James Media.

www.creativejamesmedia.com

978-1-956183-18-4 (trade paperback)

First U.S. Edition 2024

This book is dedicated to my sweet sister-in-law, Angela Guidice, and my wonderful brother, Joseph Guidice. Joey, thank you for keeping your promise.

CHAPTER 1

THE WEEKEND

IT WAS the summer before my twenty-third birthday. Micah and I had just graduated from the University of Nevada in Las Vegas, and we needed a damn vacation. Some of us—*me*—had jobs to keep, so we settled on a two-day getaway across the desert to the state line. We needed to let loose, pull out all the stops, you know, live the cliché "What happens in Vegas, stays in Vegas." Technically it was Primm, but you get the idea.

Micah had been my best friend since the first day of kindergarten; life wouldn't be the same without her.

"Hey Jess, did you find the brown suitcase?" Micah shouted from the bedroom.

"Yeah, I put it in the living room."

"The living room? Where are you?"

"The patio. I wanted to water the plants before we left. This weekend's supposed to be a scorcher, and it's not like I can ask Gideon to come over."

I'd dated Gideon Cooper for about three years. He was tall, charismatic, looked great in a pair of jeans ... and we just broke up.

"Hey, did you see my puzzle book?" Part love, part addiction, it was my fave thing to do before bed.

"Yeah, I already threw it in your bag."

"Cool, thanks!"

Making a last pass around the apartment, I checked the stove and then checked it again, turning each dial to appease the little voice in my head that they were indeed shut off.

A twinge of doubt in my gut had me tugging on each window and the patio door to be sure everything was locked up tight.

I grabbed the keys from the bowl on the side table near the front door, the two of us wheeled out our knock-off Louis Vuitton luggage.

I was struggling to cram the last suitcase into the trunk when my cell phone rang. Micah slipped it out of my back pocket and answered. Her voice grew hard, and I knew without a doubt it was Gideon. I slammed the trunk and turned around. Micah stood with her arm stretched out and the phone in her hand, with a very pissed-off look on her face. She shook her head. I grabbed the phone and walked back inside. "Hello?"

"Babe, it's me. Please don't hang up," his voice cracked.

"What do you want? I thought we settled this the other night." My heart pounded in my chest as I struggled to answer with a firm tone.

"Maybe it was settled for you, but not for me. I love you. I'm sorry a thousand times over for not seeing we were in trouble, but please, we need to talk about this. You can't just chuck three years. Can we just meet for a few minutes?"

My heart said yes, but my head said shut the hell up. "I can't. I'm leaving and won't be back until Sunday night."

"Leaving? Where are you going?"

"Primm. Me and Micah are getting away for the weekend. I'll think about it." There was a long lull of silence. This was really hurting him. Go figure, I thought I'd be the one graveling in this breakup. Not that I'm not dying a slow death inside—the sound of his voice made me want to forget the trip and drive furiously over to his house. But that's not gonna solve anything. Besides, Micah would tackle me before I reached the car, and for a skinny girl, she's pretty strong. "Gideon. You still there?"

"Yeah. Promise me we can talk when you get back?"

"I have to go."

"But babe—"

I didn't hear anything after that—I hung up.

CHAPTER 2

DESTINATION ARRIVAL

WE PULLED out onto the open freeway—wind in our hair and the promise of adventure around every corner. Okay, the wind was from the air conditioning, and the adventure was more like our hopes the car wouldn't overheat before we reached our destination. But we were driving with Vegas in the rearview, so there was that.

Gideon's call was still stinging, so Micah decided to try and rally on my side.

"He had some nerve calling you after what he did. I mean, darn, it's only been a couple of days," she said.

I glared at her. "Micah, don't. We're here to have fun. I don't want to think about him."

Micah nodded, then turned up the radio, joining in as Lady Gaga belted out her latest hit. I, on the other hand, opted to count the Joshua trees as they swooshed by. Quite the accomplishment while keeping your eyes on the road.

I'd always admired the hidden beauty of the desert. It was never exactly what it appeared to be, and that intrigued me. Life could be harsh under the glare of the summer sun, and yet, it thrived. Sometimes I felt like that with Gideon. His presence could be consuming like the sun trying to drain life from the parched desert, and yet … here I was. I guess we're stronger than we think sometimes.

I gazed up at the mountains, and the sky caught my attention. It was clear, no desert haze today. The pale blue painted across the atmosphere reminded me of the Easter eggs I'd colored with my mom as a child. Scattered puffs of white clouds could just as easily have been the tails of bunnies as they hopped through kelly-green blades looking for some tasty garden treats. It was beautiful.

I heard a gasp and turned to see Micah grinning ear to ear. In the distance, two large casinos erupted from the middle of nowhere. We had arrived in Primm.

"Look!" Micah pointed to the giant Ferris wheel. She could get excited at the simplest things. "Two days of fun and chillin. Doesn't that sound wonderful?"

I was still smarting over Gideon, but I didn't want to disappoint her. She looked so happy, like a kid tasting chocolate for the first time.

"I'm psyched. I could really use this weekend," I lied.

"I knew it. I thought at first you wouldn't be too thrilled, but I knew you'd perk up."

"Yep. I'm ready to leave everything behind and just have a total party weekend." Micah looked at me and her smile faded. Oh no—overkill.

"You don't have to humor me. I'm a big girl. If you want to sulk the whole weekend away, by all means, have at it. But don't think I'm going to indulge you. I'm having fun despite your sarcasm." Her brows knitted.

"I'm sorry. I wasn't trying to be sarcastic. I was trying to sound enthusiastic. But come on, how do you expect me to just turn it off? Cut me some slack, it's still raw."

"Okay. I'm sorry. I just want us to have a good time.

You're right, though. Truce?" I looked at her. She was just trying to make me feel better, even if I wasn't ready. I put my hand out, and she grabbed it. "Truce."

We were staying at the Primm Resort Hotel and Casino, where the concert was scheduled. I pulled up in front of the building and followed the signs to the parking garage. We unloaded our bags and trudged back to the casino entrance to check in. The large glass doors opened automatically, a much appreciated advance of our modern world. Wheeling our luggage into the lobby of the hotel, I couldn't help but notice the decaying decadence of midcentury Las Vegas.

Although Primm was much newer than many of the downtown casinos, the red, well-worn carpet, gold sconces, and gaudy crystal chandeliers mimicked the days of the Rat Pack and mob occupied Las Vegas. Micah spotted a group of kiosks, and we checked in.

"What's our room number?" I asked.

"Uh, 629. There are the elevators."

Micah pointed to a set of gold and black brocade doors, a testament to the overdone theme of most every casino I've been in.

The ride up felt more like a slow ascension into the Twilight Zone. Music from the 1950s lulled the rider to memories of sock hops and bouffant hair do's while the creaking of the pulleys suggested a destination more ominous than the sixth floor.

The ding announcing our arrival sparked a small burst of excitement. Unfortunately, the floral wallpaper pasted along the hallway to our room extinguished it. More tropic than desert, I thought it would be better suited in a cheap motel in Florida. A small table with an oversized, silk floral arrangement stretching beyond the confines of its pedestal was oddly placed a few feet away from the elevator doors. Blooms of lavender, rose, and white were a poorly chosen contrast to the jungle green and brown print serving as a background.

"Here it is," Micah swiped the key card along the side of the steel lock. "Room 629, the beginning of our two days of fun."

Thankfully, when we got inside, the room was clean, even if it was outdated. The once vibrant teal rug had dulled to a smokey blue, the matching teal and gold striped wallpaper was probably better with a few years of fading, and yet I still had to look away. The white laminate and gold-trimmed furniture might have been more comfortable in the twentieth century, but it was affordable and convenient.

Micah opened a suitcase, pulled a few items out, and turned. "Hey, there's no closet. How am I supposed to hang up these dresses so they don't wrinkle?"

I chuckled.

"What's so funny?" Her eyes widened.

"Well, you've passed it about three times already." I couldn't help but laugh. Micah is so smart, but sometimes the smallest things escape her.

"What the hell are you talking about? No, I didn't." She was standing by one of the beds.

"Walk back in line with the bathroom and look to your right. See that little alcove cut out into the wall?"

"Yeah." She was stretching her neck like a turkey being prepared for Thanksgiving dinner.

"Look closer."

"Oh, there's hangers in there." She chuckled. "I can't believe I walked by that thing and never noticed. I was looking for an actual closet." I shook my head, and we both laughed again. I walked over to the window to check out the view. Yep —definitely affordable.

"Hey. Come here and check this out."

"Why? What do you see?" She joined me, and I pointed to buildings in the desert, on the north side of town.

"Are those houses?" she asked, squinting.

"I think so, or at least that's what they look like. It's hard to tell just by the roofs."

"How come we didn't see them when we were driving in? You'd think we'd notice an entire neighborhood."

"I know it's been a while since we've come up, but they weren't there last time."

A knock at the door interrupted our little mystery.

"Who is it?" I looked through the peephole. A disheveled twenty-something stared back at me. His tousled blonde locks and five o'clock shadow belonged on the beach, surfing a few waves before a sundown chill around the firepit.

"Hotel management."

I looked over at Micah, who had a brow raised.

I opened the door no wider than my Android. "Yes, how can I help you?"

"Hello Miss, I want to apologize for any discomfort and would like to bring you to a new room."

"Discomfort? What are you talking about?"

"This room was supposed to be closed for cleaning. Apparently, the prior guest had complained about an odor."

"Nope. No smells here. We're good but thank you."

"Miss I ..."

His final words were met with a closed door.

"What the hell? I just started hanging up my clothes. Do you smell anything?" Micah sniffed.

"Whatever. Maybe the last guest was trying to wangle a free room."

"I bet you're right. My cousin who works for the Bellagio said stuff like that happens all the time."

"Hey, can we go have fun now?"

"Absolutely."

I was getting hungry, so Micah and I checked out the mall and food. We ordered the stuffed cheese-and-spinach pizza from Sbarro and sat at a table with our sodas while we waited for it to bake.

It always amazed me how many tourists came to shop at Primm. They come by the busload, most of them Japanese. I guess it's a lot cheaper to buy an upscale bag here at the outlet mall than it is in Japan. And a forty-five-minute ride from the strip is a small price to pay for designer bargains.

As malls go, the one in Primm was kind of nice. High end and discount married together under a plethora of marble, stone, and unusually wide isles.

"I'm growing old waiting for this pizza." I scrolled through my phone.

"I know, where the heck ... finally."

The guy from Sbarro's set the pizza down on the table next to our plates and red crushed pepper. His awkward half-smile tingled my nerves, and I pulled back to create distance from the greasy-haired stranger.

I made sure he was not in earshot before questioning Micah. "Did you get a vibe from that guy?"

"If you mean a creepy-and-I don't-know-why feel, then yes."

"Oh well, he's gone, and we got pizza. You want some pepper?"

"Of course. Is there any other way to eat it?"

"Nooooo," we said in unison.

Micah and I chowed down like we hadn't eaten in days, then headed to the nearest boutique for cheap accessories.

We had similar taste in clothing and colors, so we got more for our very tiny buck. We settled on two pairs of earrings, a bright blue belt, and a blue-and-cream scarf. Then we went to throw on our suits and lay by the pool for a few hours.

As we waited for the elevator, a scent tickled my nose. I

spun around to see a really cute guy standing behind us. He smelled delicious. Gideon wore the same scent most of the time. *Ouch*— a stab to the heart. I tried to let it roll off, but it grabbed me and held tight. I found myself drifting off to happier times we shared.

"Hey, are you listening to me?" Micah was shaking my arm.

"Uh, yes, I am. Okay—no. What did you say?"

"I *said,* how about we skip dinner since we had a late lunch? And after we lay out for a while, take a drive to Nipton?"

The hidden gem was a one-horse town about ten miles away. There's not much there, but Micah was a history buff, and I'm really into antiques. The small town was straight out of the Old West some one hundred years ago, so it was a win, win for both of us.

"Yeah, that sounds good." I was up for anything that took my mind off Gideon. We returned to the hotel room and changed into our bathing suits. I glanced at my reflection in the bathroom mirror, a last check to make sure everything was where it should be. I wasn't exactly Marilyn Monroe, but I was rocking some curves, and my new bronze bikini was really complimenting the olive tone I inherited from my mom.

Micah grabbed our room card off the table and took a quick look out the window.

"Jess, get the hell over here."

Micah rarely cursed.

I reached for my wrap, but she padded across the room, grabbed me by the wrist, and pulled me to the window.

"Look." She pointed to the north side of the desert.

"Look at what?" I wasn't following her at all.

"Does everything look right to you?" I meticulously scanned the landscape, but honestly, I really couldn't see what she was getting at.

"What are we looking for?"

"The *neighborhood*, it's gone."

I pushed her to the side so I could get a better look. "Impossible. Your view is blocked or something."

"The view's not blocked. It's *gone*."

She was right.

CHAPTER 3

A BLOODY MESS

WE STOOD SIDE-BY-SIDE, gaping out the window for several minutes.

"I need a drink," I said. It probably wasn't the most productive idea but … I do love a good Merlot.

We stepped out of the elevator and traipsed diagonally through gaps in the crowd gathered in front of the check-in desk.

The mass thickened, and the path to the bar was blocked. A young woman stood by the registration desk, her screams barely distinguishable from the clattering rumble of the slot machines alerting patrons to yet another near win.

Micah inched closer, but one of the hotel staff grabbed her arm and motioned her to step back. I heard a stranger's voice say they had called security, but I couldn't see them. Security in a casino is usually visible. Why they were taking so long was beyond me.

I pushed through so I could get a better look. The woman was covered in blood and stared directly into my eyes. My heart skipped a beat and then another before pounding against my chest.

"Get out! You have to get out! Now! The both of you!" She pointed to me and Micah.

I wanted to ask her what she meant, but the only thing I could muster up sounded more like a squeak than any real words. The stranger's eyes widened with each syllable that passed through her cracked lips. Beads of sweat trickled from her forehead, dropping like rain to the marble tile beneath her bare feet.

Micah inched forward, and I regained enough composure to reach for her arm. "Where you going?"

"Look at the crowd. They're enjoying the show, some of them are filming it, for god's sake."

Okay, if my BFF was gonna walk into the lion's den, the least I could do was walk with her. Maybe just a few steps behind though, you know, in case the shit hits the fan, and I can pull her back. It sounded pretty reasonable in my head.

Micah held her hand out to the desperate soul. "My name is Micah. I'd like to help. Can you tell me your name? Maybe you have someone here I can call?"

"What is wrong with all of you?" the woman screamed, her eyes growing wider as panic took over.

Security swarmed around her, and in a matter of seconds, she was gone. Silence filled my head despite the jangling bells around us.

If I hadn't needed a drink before, I did now, but my legs wouldn't listen to my brain. Apparently, Micah was experiencing the same problem. I thought about shouting to her, "Let's get the hell out of here!" but all I could do was stare at the blood-stained tiles under the woman's feet.

Additional security guards arrived and ordered the crowd to disband. Micah and I drifted mindlessly over to the bar.

We gulped our drinks before slamming them down and ordering another round. As the bartender slid a second round in front of us, Micah whispered, "Okay, what just happened?

Do you think she understood what I said? And all the blood, I mean ... son of a monkey."

It took me a minute to answer; I was still trying to process what I had just witnessed.

"Uh, well, she spoke English. Actually, she sounded like she might have come from England. So, my guess is she understood you. I don't know why she didn't respond."

Micah's gaze met mine; her usual Emerald greens had turned to forest—her telltale for fear.

I continued. "First we see those houses out of nowhere, and then poof, they're gone. Now this poor woman. What the hell was she talking about? I don't know what's going on in this place, but I think we might want to reconsider this trip and go home."

Judging by her pursed lips, we agreed. We stood to leave.

"We need to get our bags and check out." Micah was always the logical one.

"Forget it. There's nothing up there we can't live without. We should go now!"

"Jess, come on. We'll at least get our things. We can just call from the road to tell them we left early."

Sigh. "Okay, but let it be said, I think this is a bad idea."

Looking back, we should have run.

Before we reached the elevator door, a man approached us wearing a hotel badge. His chiseled chin, steel jawline, and Roman profile accented his confident posture. Framed with a thick head of wavy brown hair, he should've been attractive, but he wasn't. His GQ features were distracted by an unusually narrow head.

"You two witnessed the incident a few minutes ago, didn't you?" We nodded. "I am so sorry you had to see that." His apologetic tone sounded deep but monotone, like my phone's virtual assistant trying to fake emotions. "My name is Jonathon Smith, the hotel manager. The woman's husband explained that she had tragically suffered a miscarriage recently, and it devastated her. He tried to calm her, but she completely broke down. I hope you weren't too frightened; I heard it was very unsettling."

I looked at him and shook my head. "Unsettling? I don't think that even begins to describe it."

"I'm sorry. Your name is?"

"Jessie Marshall." This guy was annoying me, but I couldn't quite figure out why.

"Miss Marshall, I can understand your frustration. We had a fight break out in the parking lot a few minutes prior. Most of the security was outside, trying to get it under control. It is an unfortunate incident, and the hotel is truly sorry for the anguish it caused you and your friend. We would like to comp your room and offer you both a complimentary dinner."

I'm sorry to say that free trumped fear, and we turned around and headed back to the bar.

Ten men clad in white jumpsuits trimmed in rhinestones waited on the buffet line blocking the three stairs to the bar. We were serenaded with a peal of *Blue Suede Shoes* from the twilight group of Elvis impersonators as we weaved our way to a couple of vodka and 7UPs.

Even with the prospect of our free stay, we were still shaken up. Our drink at the bar had turned into three before we decided to go ahead with our original plan and drive to Nipton. We arranged for the dinner to be honored on Saturday, before the concert.

Neither one of us was really in a talkative mood, so the ten-mile drive was quiet. Well, except for the low humming from the air conditioner, which eerily fit the mood looming in the car.

The little western town felt further away than ever before. Maybe it was the fact I couldn't get that screaming woman out of my head, and I felt like screaming myself.

When we finally got to Nipton, it was late, and everything was closed except for the bar—which wasn't a bad thing. We went in to have a drink. The place was dead—the bartender preoccupied with a man sitting at the dark end of the bar. We slid into a booth, and Micah went to get us drinks.

I was, well, just trying to remain sane. This morning if you would have told me I could forget the Gideon drama that wrenched my gut over the past few weeks, I would've thought you were nice but delusional. However, everything that's happened since we got to Primm has officially blown my mind. Gideon who? I couldn't believe we decided to stay. A free room and dinner, and we're willing to forget that a town appeared then disappeared, and a woman covered in blood could be tossed aside like no big deal. Boy, did I feel like a cheap date.

I watched the bartender; he wouldn't take his eyes off the man in the dark corner. The more he studied him, the more I sized up the bartender. It was like a game of chicken. I wanted to see who would crack first, the bartender, the stranger—or me.

But when the stranger became less interested in the guy tending drinks and more interested in Micah and me, I quickly turned my head.

"Micah. Is that guy staring at us?"

"You mean the guy in the dark corner? Yeah. I noticed that too."

"Both of those guys are giving me the creeps. Look at the way the bartender keeps eyeing him. Something is definitely going on here."

"I know it's weird. Right? This has been the strangest night ever, and it's not getting any better. I say we hit the road, go back to the hotel, and go to bed. Let's close this day out before something else goes sideways."

I nodded. Plopping down on the bed in a locked hotel

room sounded way safer than a drink in a one-horse town with two glare-dueling dudes.

As we pulled into the parking lot back in Primm, my stomach growled.

"Hungry?" Micah asked.

I shook my head, eager to get to our room and hide away from the weird night. But as I did, my stomach rolled, emitting a low rumble.

"Well, I'm hungry," Micah said, climbing out of the car and slamming the door behind her.

Luckily, an all-night café was plunked down in the middle of all the bells and shiny money-sucking machines. The hostess, a tiny, white-haired lady who probably should've retired ten years ago, showed us to our seats. We piled into a sticky peach and cream leather booth. As I gazed around the room at my fellow late-night diners, my mind couldn't help but wander. The dingy turquoise and peach carpet had a Southwest flair that fell out of fashion about twenty years ago. Tiered chandeliers with antler accents hung over each table and churned my gut. Not even the soft shades of natural brown and rawhide were enough to calm the volcanic acid. I never understood the allure of displaying murdered animal parts for aesthetic pleasure.

My disapproval for the casino's choice of design was abruptly halted when a fellow late-night diner entered and slid into the empty booth across from us.

I recognized him from the bar in Nipton. He was six feet tall with dark brown hair, cut short but with a slight wave. It had been difficult to make out his eye color, but the square jawline and neatly trimmed goatee were undeniably the same. Micah gave him a sideways glance and slightly nodded. Now

I believe in coincidence, just like the next person but come on.

We squirmed in our seats when the guy leaned out, filling the empty space between us.

"Excuse me. You were at the bar a bit ago, weren't you?" *Hmm, Mr. Beautiful-but-could-be-a-serial-killer is English?*

"Yes," I managed to blurt out. "We saw you at the end of the bar. Can we help you with something?"

"I was wondering if I might have a word."

Our hero came just in time. The blonde, perky, twenty-something was as much out of place in the restaurant as I felt. With pad and pen ready, she asked to take our order.

"Well, we're about to order our food, and to be honest, we're exhausted. It's been a very unusual day."

The hue from the death chandelier cast a spotlight, accenting his tear-stained cheeks. "Yes, I know. The woman you saw in distress earlier was my wife."

CHAPTER 4

THE STRANGER

STUNNED, it took a minute before Micah blurted out, "Why the heck are you following us?"

The man sighed. "Following you? I'm here to warn you. This place isn't what it seems to be. Please, I know what I'm talking about. I'm trying to keep you safe."

"Well, you have a strange way of showing it." I could feel the heat rise from my belly. "Stalker much?"

"My intent is not to frighten you; our encounter in Nipton was a coincidence. I came over to tell you both, you need to leave."

It's funny how much better things sound with an accent. He basically said get the hell out of Dodge, but with his English twang, it was lovely. *Focus, Jessie.*

"You said that woman was your wife. What did you mean, 'was'?"

He looked down at the wedding ring on his left hand. A droplet of water cascaded down his chin, landing on the silver band.

"She passed away shortly after you saw her in the casino."

"Wait. If you were in the casino, how did you beat us to the bar?"

"I wasn't at the casino. I'd gone to Nipton searching for her. She'd been missing for a while. I hoped maybe someone had seen her. When you arrived, I had just questioned the bartender. Something felt off, so I ordered a drink." The stranger ran his fingers through his hair. "I thought if I hung out for a bit, I could engage him in more conversation, maybe figure out what he was hiding or if he was hiding anything. I didn't know who you were at the time."

"So, how did you find out we were there with your wife?"

"Right after you left, I got a call from the hotel. They told me what happened."

"That doesn't explain how you knew it was us." *This dude better get to the point, accent shmacksent, this is like riding a merry-go-round.*

"When I came into the casino, one of the cocktail waitresses recognized me and offered her condolences. She had shared a few laughs with me and my wife when we first arrived. She pointed out the two of you, telling me you had witnessed the whole thing." The stranger sat back.

Oh joy, lucky for us, you can get a clear shot of everyone in the café from the gaming floor.

I'm sorry was on the tip of my tongue, but the words stuck in my throat. Thank the heavens Micah stepped in.

"We're sorry for your loss, but ... you never told us your name."

"My name is Simon Pennwell, and my wife was Catherine."

"I'm Micah, and this is Jessie." She pointed to me. "I don't understand. What does any of this have to with us?"

Simon looked away, his gaze focusing on the hostess at the register. "It has everything to do with you ... Catherine, so many others."

He darted his attention back to us. Sadness dulled his steel-blue eyes, giving him an air of vulnerability—something I recognized and felt a kinship with. Pushing back my grief, I listened as our new acquaintance began the story that would soon become our reality.

"It was the first time either of us had left England. Catherine's sister was getting married. She was so excited to take this vacation; we both were. The wedding was splendid, and Pasadena is beautiful. We had a week of holiday left, and Catherine's new brother-in-law suggested Las Vegas. It sounded fun."

Simon stood and approached our booth. "Do you mind?"

I got up and scooted next to Micah, my cue that it was okay for him to join us. Once he was settled, he placed his elbows on the table and rested his chin on his fists. "You never know who's listening."

I found myself scooting closer to Micah, or maybe she scooted closer to me. Either way, we sat wide-eyed, shoulders touching, and captivated by Simon's mysterious tone.

"We arrived in Primm Thursday afternoon, and we were supposed to stay for only an hour. But the bus had engine trouble, and the part couldn't be delivered until morning. The tour company arranged rooms for the night." Simon shook his head. "Catherine and I stayed at a different hotel than the others."

The anxiety train sped like a bullet along my veins.

"There was a lovely blues band playing, and the hotel had given us free tickets, so we were chuffed to bits about our little detour. I wish she hadn't looked. I wish—we should have just ignored it. We *should* have just gone to the pub."

Micah jumped in. "Looked at what? What did your wife see?"

"Catherine peered out the window and noticed a little town. When we were leaving, she glanced out the window again. That's when everything changed."

He looked at us and then out into the restaurant. In a near

whisper, he uttered the words, "It was gone. The whole bloody town had disappeared."

I know it sounds ridiculous because we'd just met the guy, but I believed he really was just trying to help us. You know that little voice inside that you don't always listen to? Well, mine was screaming he's for real, and you guys should probably listen and leave. As usual, my mouth got in the way. "We saw it too."

Micah's head whipped around, and her glare suggested I was probably too forthcoming, but what the hell?

"Then you're in Room 629?"

I nodded.

He leaned his elbows on the table and then traveled his gaze to Micah. "The room—the one you're in now, room 629 —that's the one we had. When my wife questioned the front desk about what she had seen, they quickly moved us. After that, nothing was the same. Nothing will ever be the same."

Simon buried his head in his hands, and Micah reached out to him just as the waitress began wiping down the adjoining booth. Call me paranoid, but the perkiness from her original wide-eyed greeting was replaced with a shifty narrow glare. Glancing from side to side as she ran a wet cloth over the Formica tabletop, her lust for life had slowed to a flickering fade. I mean, how many times can she clean the ketchup bottle?

"Hey, maybe we should go someplace else." I nodded to the scouring scourge at the other table.

"Good idea, someplace we can talk in private. Maybe we should go to our room."

I'm not sure if Micah could tell, but I swear my jaw nearly hit the floor. Yes, I thought Simon was telling the truth, but so was Ted Bundy half the time. I squeezed her thigh under the table, and she responded with rounded eyes and a stiff lip.

This was Micah's nature, the caregiver. Once, we were at a

red light and saw a boy get hit by a car. She jumped out of the car to help and even called the hospital to check up on him—a quality I've always loved about her—until now.

The walk to the elevator felt more like the green mile rather than the means to get to our room. I swiped my palms along the side of my jeans. Not even the enormous, prismatic chandelier hanging above the poker tables was enough to distract or impress me.

The elevator felt much smaller than our earlier ride, and I think twenty-four crayons shoved into a box meant for eight best described my anxiety. I fanned my face with my hand and gasped for breath. Great, my asthma was trying to warn me. Well, you're a little late, you stupid breath-stealing disease.

Ding. A gush of cool air flooded in as the doors welcomed us to the sixth floor, relieving part of my over-imaginative nerves. I pulled my inhaler from my pocket and sucked in a lung-expanding breath. Okay. A little better.

Eyeing the hall from the steel box, I shivered. Gloom dripped from the green floral wallpaper like sap from a desert pine. It's weird how your perception can sway. Rustling for the key card in my purse, I nearly tripped when one of the hotel employees abruptly brushed by, catching my shoulder in her haste. I swear, no one has manners anymore. I wanted to make a mental note of her face, but her head was down, so she got a pass this time.

The click of the lock rung like church bells to my ears as I set my purse down on the bed and reassessed our stranger. Micah must have felt my nervous energy because she grabbed my arm and stepped back by the window, putting a comfortable space between us and our guest.

"I want coffee, anyone else?" I reached for the hotel phone on the bedside table.

"Isn't that odd?" Simon raised a brow. "There's no coffee pot in this room."

Micah looked around. "You're right, that is weird. It's like a given now. You get a wanna-be coffee bar."

"Weird yes, helpful—no." I pressed the buttons for room service and ordered a pot of nerve calming warmth.

Simon sat at the small dining table next to the door. I wasn't sure if he was consciously trying to give off a non-threatening vibe, but his relaxed demeanor—with uncrossed legs and hands neatly placed on the tops of his thighs—calmed my buzzing nerves.

Squashing the deafening silence, I blurted out, "You said you and your wife arrived last Thursday, and that's the first time she noticed the town. Where have you two been since then?"

He rounded his shoulders.

"It sounds ridiculous, but I haven't a clue. We changed our room, and then Catherine was determined to go find those houses. We rented a car first thing in the morning."

Micah and I sat on the lip of the air conditioning unit, our backs pressed against the windowsill.

"It was still dark out when we woke up, and I ordered some breakfast from room service. While my wife was in the shower, I ran down to the gift shop and bought some snacks and a few bottles of water. Catherine was so excited. An honest-to-god mystery right here for her to investigate, it exhilarated her. I, on the other hand, would have rather a day by the pool. The whole thing was odd, yes, but not enough for a bimble in the Mojave Desert."

"They should've gone to the pool," Micah murmured.

"Hindsight," I whispered.

"Simon, I don't mean to sound insensitive, but can we skip to the part about the houses? What did you find?" Micah's foot tapped; she was getting impatient.

"We drove the car as far as we could, but the terrain made it rough on our Hyundai rental. We left the vehicle and walked for about 30 minutes before we found it, no more than ten feet in front of us, a house erected in the middle of nowhere. We froze. The whole thing was quite dodgy. My first instinct was to leg it ... we should have. But the allure was too strong, especially for Catherine. We approached the front door, but as I reached for the knob—it disappeared. The entire dwelling had bleeped out of existence."

"What the hell did you do? I mean, where did you go? Who did you tell? *Did* you tell anyone? And what in God's name happened to Catherine?" I needed answers.

Simon squirmed. "I can't tell you. I just can't."

"Simon, we don't know what's going on, and you're the only one who can help us. You said you wanted to warn us. How are we supposed to know what to do if you won't help us?"

"Jessie—your name is Jessie, right?"

"Uh huh."

"I'm not trying to be difficult or hold out on any information that may help you. It's because I *can't* tell you. I want to. Believe me, if I could, I would. But after we reached the hotel room, something happened, and I can't remember a thing. We lost almost an entire week. When we woke up, we were in the basement of the casino, and Catherine was practically hysterical. Blood covered her pants, and there was a strange mark on her hip."

"Strange? How?"

"I don't know ... it was new. And sore. She could barely touch it. I tried to talk it out, thought maybe we'd spark something, but she was sputtering words that made no sense."

"What did she say?"

"It was gibberish. I'm not sure how it could help."

"Tell us what she said."

"She was crying and holding her stomach, and well, she

was saying over and over again, 'My baby, my baby.' But my wife wasn't pregnant. I'm sure of it."

"Maybe ..."

"No. I'm positive. She couldn't get pregnant."

While I waited for a cup of steamy black gold, I contemplated several scenarios for our little adventure ... none ended well.

"Hey Jess, Jess."

"Huh?"

"You're shivering. You okay?"

"I'm good. I just really need that coffee."

The sudden knock at the door brought both hope and doubt. Simon peered through the peephole.

"Your wish has been granted." His smile didn't reach his eyes.

Micah cleared space for the pot, and I graciously poured coffee for everyone. Okay, maybe more selfishly than graciously. I really wanted my cup. I could hear my mom's voice in my head pointing out the impoliteness of just serving myself the life-sustaining nectar.

Micah tasted the brew with as much enthusiasm as a dentist appointment. I, on the other hand, was so mesmerized by the caffeine fix that all questions faded from my mind.

Micah prompted Simon to continue. "You said blood covered Catherine's pants.

Where did the blood come from? I got pretty close to her, and I didn't see any cuts."

Simon put his head in his hands and shook it back and forth.

"I haven't a clue. But she said something about being in one of those houses. Maybe someone hurt her. She was confused and scared; she didn't really know what she was saying."

"She said she was in a house—one of the ones that disappeared?"

"I think."

"Simon. We need to know."

"Calm down." I hate being the voice of reason. It makes me feel like my mom. "His wife is gone. Weird shit is happening, and he has no idea where he's been for half of the goddamn week."

Simon sat back down on the chair and put his head in his hands. "No, she's right. I'm sorry. I've been so confused, and I feel like I can't go on breathing without Catherine." Micah put her hand on his shoulder. Knowing her, it was half apology ... half consoling.

Our Kumbaya moment was interrupted by three quick raps on the door.

CHAPTER 5

THE EX

MICAH SHUFFLED TO THE DOOR. She paused, took a breath, and checked the peephole. Looking over her shoulder, it wasn't fear I saw in her eyes—she was pissed. Once the divide between our room and the hallway was open, I understood why.

"Jess...," said Gideon.

I jumped up, my body stiffening with anger. How the hell could he just show up?

"Gideon, what the fuck are you doing here? Is there an issue with your brain function? I told you we'd maybe talk when I got back."

"I really needed to see you, babe." Gideon slid into one of the chairs.

"Don't get comfortable, you won't be here long. *You* needed to talk to me. That's it. It's always about you. What you're feeling, what you want."

"Jess, come on, not here in front of ... who is this guy?"

"None of your business. And I'm not the one who barged in, so, no, you don't get to choose who hears what you say."

In the past, anytime we fought, I felt like I was drowning. Gideon was always self-assured and steady. He could slide his way out of the worst situation, and never once did I see him get caught up in emotion. He knew how to get what he wanted, and I was the one to give in—not this time. Before we left Las Vegas, I promised myself, and frankly, I like keeping my promises.

"Five minutes, please."

"Let's go in the hall."

Micah crossed her arms. "I don't think that's a good idea."

"I'll be okay. If you hear a terrifying scream, just come and rescue him." I smirked.

"Great. Make a joke" Poor Micah. I shouldn't have said that. She's tough on the outside with a double helping of mush on the inside.

"We'll go in the bathroom."

Micah managed a half-smile, but I swear the grip on her crossed arms was cutting off the blood flow.

"Come on, the porcelain awaits."

I refused to sit on the toilet, so my bum rested on the edge of the tub, leaving the waste throne for a befitting king.

Gideon knitted his brow. "What the frig is going on? Who's the strange guy?"

"This is what you ask me after pleading for alone time? You've got to be kidding."

He tapped his fingers on his thumbs like notes to song, his OCD telltale.

"I made an appointment with a counselor. My issues ... I can't let them ruin what's between us."

I think the gape in my mouth could've housed an airplane. Before we split, he said he loved me, and I was the only one for him. But his love for himself sometimes overruled his feelings for me. An insatiable need to be social media's next big influencer kept a phone in his hand, camera-ready of course, and a toothy grin on his face. Let's just say I'm hesitant to buy in on the overnight change.

"I'm happy for you, but that doesn't instantaneously make things better between us."

"I know."

"I got bigger issues right now, and this, whatever this is, is gonna have to wait."

His gaze traveled from my eyes to the floor. He nodded; no rebuttal passed his lips.

"Are you in trouble?"

"I'm not sure. I think so."

Relaxing the vice grip on my shoulders, I gave him a recap of the day, the town, Simon, and Catherine.

I didn't have a clue how he might react to my day. Astonishment, which I could have dealt with, or maybe disbelief. Maybe even saying, "You're crazy, Jess." But there was nothing. He just sat there like it was storytelling time at the local library.

His expressionless response took me aback.

"Hey. Did you hear what I've been telling you? Say something—anything."

"I believe you."

I was completely baffled. Even *I* had a tough time believing me.

"You believe me, just like that? No questions, no objections? I don't even know what to do with that."

He leaned forward.

"I believe you because I saw them, too."

"You saw what?"

"The houses. I saw the houses."

"What the hell are you saying? What do you mean you saw the houses? When?"

"Last year when I came up with Sam for that charity bike ride. We were off-roading through the desert and got turned around. Sam was checking out the map when a glare caught my eye. No more than fifty feet away, in the middle of the desert, was a neighborhood. Ten seconds later, it was gone."

"Gone how?"

"Just puff, not there. I never said anything because it sounded too crazy."

"We saw them. Me, Micah, Simon, and his wife. She told Simon she was *in* one of those houses. She's dead now."

"Dead? Jeez, Jess. Was she able to tell anyone what she saw?"

"I don't know. Simon was telling us the story when you knocked on the door. You have lousy timing."

"Yeah, I hear that. More and more lately."

I could hear the desperation in his voice, but there wasn't time. We had to find out what was going on and get the hell out of here.

"Let's just go back out there so Simon can finish his story. And don't think I'm letting this slide. You had no business coming out here."

"I know, but—"

"No. You had no right. We'll talk about it later." There were too many things going on. Gideon Cooper would have to wait—something he was definitely not accustomed to.

The wallpaper was louder than any conversation between Simon and Micah. She had positioned herself in front of the window to whatever wonderland lay out there waiting, while Simon steadily scrolled through pictures of Catherine on his phone. Micah's scrunched brows were ringing disapproval of Gideon's presence, but honestly, he was small potatoes compared to murder, death, kill.

"Simon, you said Catherine was in one of the houses. Where were you?"

"We were together. Or at least, I thought we were. We woke up almost a week later in the basement of the casino. I have no idea what happened after we got into our hotel room. It's all bits 'n bobs."

"I say we leave. I don't think we can trust security or anyone else here. Simon, we can take you to Vegas with us. We'll talk to Metro police, let them come out and investigate this shit."

"Good idea," Micah agreed.

"I still feel like I'm racing to catch up, but it makes sense to go," Gideon interjected.

How cute. He thinks his opinion matters.

"Simon, we can go to your room together."

"Yeah, we shouldn't separate." Micah bit her lower lip.

"No. Everything I need is in my pockets. I don't want to risk it. They might be waiting for me." Simon patted his back pocket.

"What are we waiting for?" Micah threw her open suitcase onto the floor in front of the honey oak dresser. Pulling an armload of clothes from each drawer, she dropped it into the gaping suitcase before moving on to the next drawer. When they were all emptied, she ran into the bathroom and returned with her toiletries bag, chucked it onto the pile before folding the bag closed. After a quick glance around the room, she nodded. "Let's go."

Luckily, I hadn't been as attentive to unpacking as my BFF. I grabbed my stuffed Louis wanna-be, the keys from the nightstand, and was ready.

We poured into the hall, bumping into each other and shuffling in a tight group, aimed for the elevators. Our heads bobbed as we scoured the hallway for anyone other than ourselves. The place was dead, but the weirdest thing caught my eye, all the rooms had brown doors with red numbers, but ours—steel grey with the black 629 smack in the center—stood out like a beacon in the fog. I shrugged my shoulders, a mystery for another day.

Micah pressed the down button, and I leaned my back against the wall. I'm so not a fan of elevators. You're either waiting forever or barely catching it before the doors shut. I'm a stairs girl myself.

"Is it me, or does this damn car move slower than molasses?"

Micah glanced at her naked wrist. "It's only been a few seconds."

"Funny."

"I try."

I'm not sure if I was preoccupied with getting out of this bizarre place, but a subtle blanket of calm quieted the anxiety burning in my stomach. Just a few more minutes, and we'd be on our way back to Vegas and closer to safety.

And then Simon said something that would change our lives forever. "I'm going back out there."

Well, that was short-lived. I grabbed my gut.

"In the name of the gods, what are you talking about?" He was obviously delusional with grief. I wanted to slap him upside the head but opted for a more subtle approach.

"You can't go back out there! What's the matter with you?" I balled my hands into tight fists. "Listen, we don't know you very well. Okay, hell, we don't know you *at all*. But the last thing you need to do is to go out there and very possibly get yourself very, very dead."

"I understand what you're saying, but she was my wife. I was supposed to protect her, and I failed her. I have to find out what happened."

"Simon—"

"Jessie, I'm going. The rest of you bloody well better get yourselves as far away from here as possible. But this is something I have to do."

I didn't hear anyone volunteer to stay, so getting out of there sounded pretty good to me. But then my lips started moving, and I could hear the words coming out of my mouth.

"You can't do this alone. I'll stay." What was I saying? My stupid emotions were taking over when my brain should be giving all the orders. Oh crap, *this* is how I get myself into so much trouble. "You'll need help, and if something goes wrong, who will know? I'll stay with you. Gideon and Micah can go back to Vegas and talk to the police."

Judging by Micah's tight jaw and wrinkled forehead, she didn't approve. I can't blame her. I didn't approve either.

Gideon shook his head.

"There's no way you're staying alone with this guy. If you're so determined, then I'm staying too."

I wanted to argue and tell him he had no say over what I did or didn't want to do. But fear kicked in, and the only thing I could get out was, "Okay."

Micah tapped the temple of her head and then walked over to the small table with the freakishly large floral arrangement. She sat on a single chair that complemented the weird placement of furniture in the hallway. "I'm staying, too."

Our little band of merry idiots was interrupted by the loud double ding of the waiting chariot. Piling into the empty car, I struggled to swallow past the lump in my throat making way for a vomit of words.

"Okay, Simon, what's the plan?"

"We casually walk through the casino and out to the desert."

"What? That's not a plan. A plan has multiple steps. Walking through the casino is a thing." I huffed.

Simon bowed his head and clasped his hands on the back of his neck. "Okay. Then...one of you brings the luggage to your car, and meets us at the sidewalk in front of the casino. Now it's a plan.

Anyone got any other ideas?"

I had nothing, and judging by Micah and Gideon's sealed lips, they had nothing either.

"Good?" Simon looked at me with a sideways glance.

I shook my head as I bit the inside of my cheek. "Yup."

CHAPTER 6
SOMEBODY'S WATCHING

LATE NIGHT CHECK-INS packed the lobby. I weaved my way through an obstacle course of suitcases, rude *no I won't get out of your way* guests, and several out-of-control toddlers. I mean, honestly, who brings kids to a casino? I've never understood the concept.

I eyed the first sign of freedom from this adult wonderland. The revolving doors glistened under the canopy of bold lights at the casino entrance. Like a marquee on Broadway, it would lead us to the next act in our little creep show.

As I passed a slot machine clanging loudly with sirens announcing a big payout, I took notice of the winner. Most would lose their shit if they hit for a hundred bucks, but a score like this should've had this little, blue-haired lady dancing in the isles. Instead, she showed no emotion as her eyes moved from the machine to meet my gaze. For a brief second, our eyes locked and I swear the chill from her glare nearly put me in my grave.

"You guys, is it me, or does the air feel a little off here?"

I glanced at the entrance again. Three barrel-chested

guards stood shoulder to shoulder, their thick necks barely visible under their steel jawlines.

"Look, I think we're being watched." I nodded toward a lanky senior standing with a cane against the wall. The guy had abandoned any attempt to be stealthy, his gaze fixated on our every move.

Simon tugged at my sleeve, and we all followed him to a row of penny slots—the machine of choice for locals looking to win big bucks for literal pennies. He weaved us through the menage of one arm bandits to a small out cove in front of the restrooms.

"I would say our casual exit has gone all to pot." Simon's eyes shifted from side to side.

"Did you see the goons at the door?" I craned my neck to see if they were still there, but the entrance was blocked by a sea of poker machines.

"I think we should stay," said Gideon.

"And do what?" Micah's laser glare must have burned its way to Gideon's insides because he shifted from side to side like a small child waiting for the bathroom.

"Calm our heels." Gideon furrowed his brow.

"He's right." Simon's shoulders dropped. "Let's go to the bar and get a drink. We have no idea why we're in their crosshairs, but we are."

"And what? Throwing back a few will fix everything?"

"No, Jessie, but it will give us time to assess our next move."

"I'll run the luggage back up to the room. Jess, give me the key card." Gideon opened his hand.

The hair on the back of my neck stood at attention, sending a cold tingle down my spine. The warning system everyone has and rarely listens to. My instinct was to run. Push our way past the mutant army at the door, hop in the car and go. Forget about Simon's quest, leave the unknown buried in

Primm, but like so many other times before, I ignored the red flag my body was waving. I handed Gideon the key, and followed my friends to the bar.

On any other day, I would've ogled the dimpled chin, sandy brown-haired beauty behind the bar. His muscles seeping out from under his short sleeve, V-neck T-shirt admittedly caught my eye for a minuscule of a second, but then so did the overly giddy couple stealing glances at us from the other end of the bar.

I kicked Micah's foot and tilted my head in their direction. She's my bestie since forever, and she speaks Jessie. Casually dropping her napkin, she scooted off the stool, and as she stood with her prize in hand, she got a good look at them.

Leaning into my shoulder, she whispered, "This is really getting creepy."

"I'll say, I don't think it could be any weirder."

I was wrong.

"How are my favorite guests? Enjoying your stay?"

I recognized the baritone voice as that of manager Jonathan Smith. The three of us spun around in our seats. Like a robot on pause, his stiff posture and blank stare stole a few beats from my heart.

Dressed in an off-the-rack designer suit, he wore shoes that were at war with the clean lines of his heather grey ensemble. Covered with dust, they looked more like Walmart than Ralph Lauren.

He came close to me—too close. I felt like I was sharing the same stream of oxygen with the cool as a freezer hotel manager. The foul aroma of onions and grease permeated his breath. Luckily, Gideon arrived in time to wedge out space between Smith and me.

"Miss Marshall. I'm glad to see you and your friends decided to stay and enjoy yourselves. Especially after that terrible incident yesterday." A small dribble of saliva pooled in the corner of his mouth. Reaching for a nearby cocktail napkin, he patted it dry. "Excuse me, Mr. Pennwell, that sounded much too callous. How are you getting along?"

Simon clenched his jaw, and I interjected before he clocked the manager. The last thing we needed was to draw even more attention.

"Thank you so much, Mr. Smith," I said, trying to keep the sarcasm out of my voice. "You and the hotel management have been very kind to us." He looked genuinely pleased with himself.

"We were just about to head over and enjoy our comped dinner before the concert." I took a few steps.

"Well, you have an enjoyable time. I'll be sure to let them know there will be four in your party instead of two. And if you or your friends need anything, please call."

"Oh, you've been so good to us already. We couldn't possibly bother you. Have a good evening." I nudged Gideon in the arm and motioned for him to go.

For the first time since we arrived, the orchestra of bells and gongs from winning slots annoyed me. Like picking the color polish at the salon and realizing once it's on your nails, you hate it, I could feel the irritation turning annoyance into anger. The further we navigated into the belly of the casino, the more obvious it became we were the sole focus.

The flaming redhead, wearing a shape-hugging, black, sleeveless dress, sat at the poker table sneaking peeks as she pretended to look at her cards, while a gangly thirty-something guy playing roulette kept one eye on the wheel and the other on yours truly. It was becoming very obvious we were about as welcome as a distant relative after you won the lottery.

Once we left the casino, Micah wandered to a remote corner of the parking lot and sat . She looked up at the three of us. Her cheeks reminded me of a couple of Fuji apples.

"Hey, you okay? You're really flushed." I sat next to her.

"Yeah. I just needed air. That was the weirdest thing in there."

"I'd say we passed weird, and we're working our way up to fucking bizarre."

"Whatever, that fruit loop Smith is all kinds of strange. I say the sooner we get some answers for Simon, the sooner we get the hell out of here."

"Did you just curse? I'm without words."

"I might say a few more before this little adventure is over, so get used to it."

"Who are you, and what have you done with my BFF?"

"Oh, shut up. Come on, let's go."

The guys were waiting on a grassy oasis at the edge of the property, a few feet before the highway.

"You okay?" Gideon questioned Micah.

I thought she'd have a salty answer, but surprisingly she just nodded.

Simon waved his hand. "Let's get out of here before someone spots us. I'll lead the way to where Catherine and I first came upon the houses."

We followed him across the highway. The indigo sky, replacing the last remnants of orange and gold, did little to ease the desert heat. Several semi-trailer trucks idled in the lot. Primm was a popular stop for truckers looking for a night's rest, a good meal, and some action on the tables.

Usually, they drew about enough attention from me as a fly circling my ice-tea. I'd mentally swat them away, not knowing who they were or where they were going. But tonight was different. I found myself looking over my shoulder, wondering if they were looking back.

We hit the desert and walked for what felt like an eternity. It had grown dark, and the shadowed mountains surrounding us took on the shape of a creature waiting patiently to pounce. I felt like the final girl in a horror movie. Only I wasn't sure if I was the savior or the sarcastic sidekick who bites it just before the real hero emerges.

Simon came to a standstill and surveyed the area. It was difficult to get a clear view. He was the only one who had been able to get a flashlight, and the half-moon provided only a minimal glow. His head dropped, and he bent down, taking in a fist of sand. He let the grains pass through his finger. "This is where my life ended." Wiping away a tear, he uttered in a cracked voice, "She was my world."

We waited. Sometimes silence is more painful than confrontation.

Breaking the somber mood, Simon stood and announced he needed to pee. Deciding his need for illumination was greater than ours, he kept the flashlight and scurried to a patch of sagebrush. He was only gone for a few moments when we heard him call out.

Micah was the first to reach him. "Oh my God!"

"What the fuck is going on?" huffed Gideon, "What are you yelling ... never mind."

Plain as day, right in front of us, smack dab in the center of nowhere, I counted ten houses. The windows were dark, with no sign of light from within. The dust caked on the panes told the same story as the weeds growing in front of the door—an indication that nothing had lived there for a long time.

"Did you see that?" Gideon pointed to the last house in the row.

"What was it?" Simon leaned in.

"A flash of light coming from inside that end house. I'm gonna walk down and take a look." I know Gideon can take care of himself, but this was different. Breakup aside, I loved him. To think of anything bad happening to him left my heart dry of blood.

"I'm going with you," I said. Completely convinced there

wasn't anything positive coming from this, I did it anyway. At least we'd be together. Love is a strange thing.

To my relief, Micah and Simon followed. Clumped together like nachos on a plate, we crept slowly, eyes and ears straining with each rustle from the unknown. The knots in my neck tightened the closer we got to our target, barely winning over the frenetic pounding in my chest. Micah's head bobbed back and forth like she was sitting in the back row of a concert, while Gideon's fists were balled up and ready for action. Only Simon remained focused on the prize, not allowing nature to distract him.

He was the first one to reach the front door. *Locked.*

Gideon took out his utility knife and inserted it into the lock. It was a Christmas gift from me two years ago, and he's carried it with him ever since.

"At least you figured out how to hold on to that." I hissed at him.

Gideon didn't even look at me. We heard a click, and without hesitation, he turned the knob, inching the faux cherry wood ajar he peeked in before pushing it wide open.

The interior was dark, but from what I could tell, it looked like a normal living room. A three-cushion, black leather sofa lined one of the walls with a matching love seat across the room. Two glass and chrome end tables adorned with textured cream, ceramic lamps crowned with square black shades screamed modern luxury. Through a doorway, a white, rectangular table perched on a thick, chrome base and six high back, white chairs with black leather seating stood in the shadow of a towering, glass front, white hutch.

Our bizarro journey had just reached a new level—a perfectly normal-looking house planted in the middle of nowhere. Jesus Christmas, what was going on?

Micah moved ahead of us to the kitchen. Stainless steel appliances glared in the beam of Simon's flashlight before it swept across the white and grey marble countertops. Suddenly, she stopped. We all took her cue and froze. Someone—no, *something* was moving around in the shadows.

Simon crept behind Micah, then grabbed her waist and gently pulled her back. Gideon sidled up beside me, one hand sliding across my palm as he wrapped his hand around mine. I glared and yanked away from him.

I turned my head just in time to see my BFF and Simon clamoring my way and what looked like—hell, I'm not sure what *it* looked like, following behind them. Gideon grabbed my hand again. This time, I let him, and we booked it for the door.

We barreled through the dining room and into the living room. But—the door! Where was the door? No. This wasn't right. There was *no* front door.

Frantic, Gideon shouted. "Go out a window!"

Micah circled the room, mumbling, "No, no, no."

"What the bloody hell? Where did it go?" Simon rapped on the wall.

Go ... help Simon. What the hell was I thinking? Five minutes, that's all I need. We just go back in time five minutes so I can tell them what a fucking bad idea this is, and we should just go home.

We clung to each other in the center of the room. I wanted to disappear into the darkness, let it engulf me. But I couldn't ignore the silhouette ten feet away, gliding silently from side to side, eyeing us with unwavering intensity.

I prayed we'd be able to find a way out. "Anybody got any suggestions? I'm wide open for some ideas."

Gideon spoke in a barely audible whisper, "Look. Over there. Stairs. Maybe we can make our way to the second floor and get out through a window from one of the bedrooms."

"You're assuming there's still windows up there." I shuddered.

"I don't know if there is or isn't. But I do know we can't just stay here. Agreed?"

"Agreed. Let's get the hell out of here." On the very quiet count of three, we all made for the stairs. None of us stopped to look back. I figured if we could outrun that thing, we'd at least make it to one of the rooms, and if the gods were with us, it'd have a lock.

Micah and I ran into the first open door, the guys tight on our heels. Gideon slammed the door shut as the terrifying echo of nails scraping along the hallway planks grew closer.

The guys pushed every bit of furniture in front of the door. Unless our stalker had the ability to move things with its mind, I didn't think that door was budging.

Wait, what if it does *have the ability to move things with its' mind? Okay, Jessie, slow down. Becoming hysterical is not exactly what you need to do right now.*

I swear that damn thing read my mind. Straight out of a scene from one of my fave movies, *The Conjuring,* smaller pieces of furniture fell away and sailed across the room, slamming into the wall raining showers of splintered wood. The heavier pieces, like a triple acrylic dresser, screeched as they slowly crept along the parquet floor. *Crap! Are you kidding me?*

Gideon and Simon went for one of the three windows, throwing aside the heavy drapes. Gideon jerked on the window several times, slamming his palm upward into the pane before he pushed up, groaning with effort. Simon joined him, and they managed to slide the window open enough for any one of us to push our way through. Freedom was a jump away.

Hope quickly betrayed us as the damn thing slammed shut, and then, I don't know how this happened, blended over the wall like wet paint before instantaneously drying to a smooth surface. The window was gone.

Micah broke down.

"This is insanity. What the hell is going on? What the hell is that thing, and what kind of twisted pile of shit is this house?" Simon tried to comfort her by pulling her closer to him, but Micah was on a roll. "Don't even waste your time with the other windows. Look, they're gone too!"

"Look!" Gideon pointed to a fairly large vent in the ceiling at the far corner of the room. The guys pulled off the cover, and Micah and I exchanged a do-or-die glance. It was dark and as hot as a sauna, but it was better than being trapped in that room waiting to be dinner. I reached out to feel the wall, anything that could help me *see* where we were but even with my arms stretched out to full capacity, I didn't hit anything.

The boys followed, and when we were all together, Gideon took his phone from his pocket.

"Hey, where's the flashlight?" I asked.

"I dropped it when I jumped up into the vent." Simon frowned.

"It's not working." Gideon kept swiping his thumb across the screen.

I pulled mine out of my pocket and Micah tried hers—nothing. The screens were black.

"What the hell?" I tapped the screen.

"Wait..." Gideon reached into his front pocket. "This should work."

He waved a lighter in front of him—we all gasped as the pale flame illuminated our surroundings.

"Okay, I don't know what *this* place is, but it doesn't look like any crawl space or attic I've ever seen," I said. "I mean, we could fit an easy a hundred people here. It doesn't make any sense. It's twice the size of the house. How is that even possible?" We continued to fumble through the very dimly lit room. I stepped gingerly, using my toes to reach out into the dark to minimize the risk of tripping. With each step, I was farther from the faint sepia glow of the Zippo.

What I could see reminded me of an operating room. An ominous examining table fitted with straps sat beneath a huge dome light. Several instruments were neatly arranged on stainless steel counters. I wasn't sure what kind of tools they were or what they were used for, but my imagination was going wild.

"We need to get the hell out of here," Gideon said.

"Really?" I raised a brow. "Because I was thinking maybe we should stay and wait for that *thing* to catch up with us. Who knows, maybe it'll give us a tour?"

Gideon sighed.

I turned to the others. "Why don't we split up and search for a door?" Everyone nodded.

Gideon tried to hold the lighter up as best he could to give a little guidance, but mostly we felt our way around the walls. The room grew warmer, and droplets of sweat trickled off my forehead. I grabbed the end of my shirt to wipe my face, but some dripped into my eye. It burned like a mother.

"Damn, that stings."

"You okay?" Micah asked.

"Yeah."

Gideon approached. "Here, let me help." He lifted a corner of his shirt and gently wiped at my eye.

"Thanks." *Why did I whisper that?* For an awkward second, our eyes linger, and then Gideon clears his throat and turns, holding up the lighter. A portion of the wall caught my attention. Like skipping stones in a pond, the walls rippled. If it wasn't solid, maybe it was a way out.

I tapped Gideon on the arm and pointed to the wall. He moved the lighter closer, slowly gliding the flame around the anomaly.

"A doorway?" I whispered.

"Where?" Micah's voice trembled.

I waved them over.

"Ouch!" Gideon shook his hand.

"Hey, where's our light?"

"It got really hot."

Dropping to his knees, he fumbled around for a few seconds. "Got it. Crap, it's still warm."

Waiting for the metal to cool down, I felt a little like I did on my first day in kindergarten. You really want to get the day started, but a part of you just wants to crawl under the covers and hide from the world. I really wanted to get out of here but was scared to death where this possible doorway would lead us.

"Okay, it's cooler, here." He handed me the Zippo and click, we had a flame.

Gideon cautiously reached out his hand to touch the wall. A protective instinct kicked in, and I grabbed his arm, pulling it back. "You can't do this. It's not safe. You have no idea what's going to happen when you touch it."

I flipped the lid on the lighter, extinguishing the flame.

"Fuck, that thing gets hot quick."

"Here, give it to me." Simon reached out and took the lighter.

"Gideon ..."

"What other choice do we have? This could be our way out. Listen, do you hear that? That thing is on its' way up here, and I know you don't want a face-to-face with it any more than I do."

What could I say? He was right. I took the lighter back from Simon and positioned it in front of the wall.

Slowly Gideon put his hand out. When he touched what should have been solid plaster, his hand passed right through. Methodically, he pushed his body through to the unknown. In a second, he was gone. We all waited, holding our breath. It wasn't long before he reappeared, but it sure felt like it.

Gideon looked fine as he came back through the wall, everything intact and a smile on his face. He grabbed my hand, and I shut my eyes. The next thing I knew, I was standing in the middle of the desert. I spun around to see the houses; they were now fifty yards away. I turned to ask Gideon what the hell, but he was gone.

I stood in the dark desert, longing to see anything normal —like casino lights across the highway. More than anything, I wished we were at the concert having fun with no knowledge of this stupid creepy place. There was a tap on my shoulder— Micah. Simon was the last to arrive, and without a word, we ran toward the lights and civilization.

We reached the casino lobby, covered in dust and breathing heavily from the run and the fear that drove it. We headed directly to what Simon referred to as the pub and ordered shots. Chugging them back, we slammed our glasses on the bar and ordered another.

We sat there for a few minutes, contemplating our brush with death. My mind was trying to process everything that had happened. I know my brain was like a lump of mush and needed a few more drinks before I could form a word. Nothing felt real, more like I was in a nightmare, and pretty soon, I'd wake up in my bed back in Las Vegas. My eyes traveled from the hunky bartender to the spread of gamblers. They had no clue what was happening. I squinted to block out the glare; casinos are always too bright.

"I don't know what the hell just happened or what that thing was. But I am really, really scared." Micah put her head on the bar and covered it with her hands. I stroked her hair to comfort her, but I don't think I was very reassuring. I needed some comforting of my own.

She lifted her head. "We need to get out of here, Jess. All of us need to go and get as far away from this creepy miserable little place as we can. Once we get back to Vegas, we can tell someone, like the police or the FBI. Anybody who can help. But we can't keep doing this on our own—we can't." She was right. But given what we saw, I wasn't so sure it was gonna be that easy.

"All right. Let's get back to the room where we can talk and check out Elm Street from the window." I was trying to be funny, but I don't think anyone was in the mood. We all slid off the bar stools and headed for the elevator. Micah pressed the button for our floor, and I gazed over my shoulder, checking our backs for any unwanted guests. I saw Smith headed our way.

"Crap. Crap. Hurry already." I tapped my fingers along the side of my legs.

Gideon grabbed my waist. "It's okay. We'll be in the room in a minute."

"No, it's not okay! Look who's coming." I pointed.

"Shit." Gideon nodded to Simon, who peered over his shoulder.

"Bloody hell."

The elevator doors opened with a familiar ding. We piled in at lightning speed, and Micah was pushing buttons before we had a chance to think. We stopped at the fourth floor, the fifth, and finally the sixth. I didn't think it was possible for human beings to move so quickly. We raced down the hall and were in the room with the door locked before I even had a chance to exhale. I collapsed on the bed with Micah right next to me. The boys sprawled out on the chairs.

We lay there for a moment before Simon broke the silence.

"We can't stay in this room for long. Smith undoubtedly will be up here in a few minutes. We need to go back out to the desert."

We all shot up and looked at him in disbelief.

"Are you out of your damn mind? We were almost killed out there, and now you want to go back?" I furrowed my brow.

"I know it sounds crazy. But I don't think we're going to be free of this unless we find out what's going on. I need to find out for my wife, and I think your lives will remain in jeopardy until we can figure who or what that thing is. Those houses are there for a reason, and something tells me we aren't the only ones at risk here."

Gideon shook his head and started pacing. "Simon's right. But there's no need for all of us to go. You two go back to Vegas. Tell the police what's going on. Simon and I will go and see if we can figure out what the hell this is all about."

"Have you gone completely insane?" I cried. "You can't go back there, and neither can Simon. We all need to get the hell out of this place, get help and let them come back and handle it. Last time I checked, Gideon, there was no badge attached to your shirt." I was so frustrated I could have punched him in the head.

"Jess, listen—"

"No. You're not going to convince me this time. This is an insanely bad idea."

He came over beside me and touched my face. *He's going to do it to you again.* Every time Gideon held my face, he could melt even the strongest conviction I might have, and he knew it.

"We're all in danger. But if you both leave now, you might have a chance to get help. Simon's not backing down, and he can't go it alone."

"Then I'm staying and going back with you." What the hell was I saying? I wanted to put my hand across my mouth, but my arm wouldn't cooperate.

"No. If something were to happen and I couldn't protect you—"

"You're not my keeper. I'm going, and I'll protect myself. End of discussion." *Now I know I'm crazy. Who runs toward the creepy unknown? Oh yeah, that would be the one in the slasher movie that is the first to die.*

"I'm scared half to death, but if Jess is staying, then I am too. I'm not leaving her here," Micah slipped a hair tie from her pocket and pulled her hair back in a ponytail. "I think we'll be stronger together. Besides, I'm not sure the police would believe us anyway. We need proof."

I gazed out the window mulling over what comes next— my answer couldn't have been clearer. In a blink, one of the houses illuminated. Someone had turned on the lights.

CHAPTER 7

THE DESERT

GIDEON CAME up with a plan to get us out of the hotel. First, we would go to the ABC store for supplies. Flashlights and possibly something we could use to defend ourselves. I seriously doubted the store stocked AK-47s, but maybe I could find a really heavy paperweight for bashing something in the head. *Think positive.* Fortunately, the store was inconspicuous, tucked away in the north end of the casino.

The hallway was one closed door away, and as I turned the lock, the cold steel felt like death between my fingers. With a deep breath, I willed my racing heart to slow and stepped out of the room with Micah and the others behind me. Waiting at the end of the hall with his arms stiff to his sides was Jonathan Smith.

Leather and jasmine tickled my nose as Gideon butted up behind me, his words grazed my ear. "Simon and I will keep him busy while you two get out of here. Meet us in the store."

I reached my hand around and rubbed my thumb along his lower back. He leaned in and whispered, "Be careful."

"Hey, just the person I wanted to talk to." Gideon waved to Smith. "If you're not busy, Simon and I have some questions for you."

Smith cleared his throat and straightened his back. "Were you leaving?"

"No guy, you see luggage? We were headed downstairs, thought we'd get our gambling on. Simon here needs some distractions if you know what I mean."

Simon pressed the button for the elevator and peered up at the light as it climbed to our floor.

Micah and I held hands and slipped past the guys with our heads down, giving no attention to the creepy manager. My clammy palm nearly slipped away from hers, and I squeezed a little tighter. My chest pounded, and I held my breath as the ding of the elevator echoed through the hall. I was sure it would grab Smith's attention. I swallowed hard to push back the lump in my throat.

"Ladies, we'll join you at the Mega Bucks slots in a few minutes."

Luckily, the gods were on our side, and the doors closed before Smith had a chance to say anything. I leaned back against the wall, taking in a deep breath. I closed my eyes until my heart gradually slowed. A rush of euphoria caused my limbs to shake, and I pressed deeper into the steel to steady my balance. The small jolt butterflied through my belly, and when the doors opened, I'd never been so happy to see a casino.

Micah and I went straight to the ABC store. I was right, definitely no AK-47s, but I did find a miniature baseball bat. Not trusting our phones would work we grabbed four flashlights, water, and snacks. It was getting close to the Fourth of July, so there were some fireworks for sale. Micah grabbed a large handful.

"Excellent choice." Gideon grinned.

"Hey, that was fast." I set our goods on the counter.

"Yeah, I didn't wanna waste too much time, didn't want to risk getting stuck."

Simon grabbed a handful of protein bars and a backpack

from across the aisle and added them to my pile. He whipped out a credit card and paid for the whole lot.

"I could've got it." I smiled.

"I know." Simon swept everything off the counter into the pack and slung it across one shoulder. "Ready?"

"Nope," I said as we fell into step behind him.

Once we were clear of the canopy of casino lights, it was blindingly dark. Buffalo Bills, the only other hotel for ten miles, was under restoration and dark for the next ten days. The closer we got to our phantom neighborhood, the more my brain spun. What the hell were we gonna do when we got there? I hoped the answers would come to us when we needed them. We kept our flashlights off to avoid drawing attention. The sky filled with stars, and on any other night, I would have marveled over the beauty. But tonight, they just were—dots.

The guys lagged a few steps behind me and Micah, and as I glanced over my shoulder, I couldn't help but wonder what poor Simon must be thinking. The little I knew about him told me he was a good guy, and to have his entire world ripped away, and in a strange country, it had to be mind-numbing. Gideon walked with confidence, always looking ahead, never down at the ground. It made him strong. But he took risks, and that made me worry. I mean, I was worried about all of them.

When we were a safe distance away from the casino and the hotel, we switched on our flashlights. In the glow, the desert landscape appeared even more ominous. Plenty of dangers hide behind the benign facade of the Mojave, making it treacherous if you should find yourself stranded in it.

My nerves were on high alert.

As I inched my way closer to danger and possibly death, I couldn't help but think of Catherine. She must have been frightened out of her mind and felt so alone. We'd just stared at her that day in the casino. We didn't do anything to help her. A wave of guilt washed over me, and I clutched Micah's arm. Her gaze met mine, her weary eyes trying to smile for me, but I knew what was behind them ... doubt.

We kept walking in the direction of the houses, but after about thirty minutes, hope was ushered away by despair. The lights that were visible just an hour ago were nowhere.

"Anyone else want a break?" Gideon wiped the back of his neck.

"Sounds good." Micah tugged at her Anthropologie sale rack T-shirt and blew down the front of her chest.

We gathered in a half-circle, facing the journey ahead. The waxing Gibbous sparsely illuminated the endless monotony of sand, brush, and more brush. The faint outline of the surrounding mountains was the only visual cue we had to orient ourselves with. We hoped if we stayed within the confines of their shadow, eventually, we would find the spot. Simon unzipped his backpack and spilled out four bottles of water. We each grabbed for one, and after our dry throats had been relieved, conversation flowed more easily.

"Okay, so we find the house with the light on, assuming it's still on, and then what?" I switched my gaze from one doe-eyed friend to the next. Let's just say I wasn't feeling oodles of confidence.

Simon interjected. "We go inside and see where it leads us. The other house took us to that creature and the weird attic; maybe this one will bring us to answers."

"And if not? Then what?"

Simon let a heavy sigh and lay back in the sand. Staring up at the sky, he murmured, "Then we leave. I'll go with you to Las Vegas."

The three of us nodded in agreement.

I took a long swig from my not-so-cold thirst quencher; too bad it couldn't squelch the burning in the pit of my stomach. There was a chance we might not make it...maybe me, maybe Simon—maybe all of us. A chill ran along my spine. *Damn*, I wish none of us had ever come.

Simon got up and brushed off his pants and shirt. "Ready, mates?"

"Jess," Gideon said. I tried to ignore him. "Can we just talk for a second?"

Micah and Simon put some space between us, and against my better judgment, I bit. "What?

"I don't know what's going to happen tonight, and I can't let it go without telling you something. The reason I drove here was to make sure you know exactly how I feel. I know my actions make you feel like I don't care and that I can be a real ass. I don't mean to."

"You should have saved yourself the trip. I've heard this shit before."

"Let me finish, please. I know I've put you through hell. All I really want is for you to be happy. And if being apart is what makes you happy, then I'll stop calling. But I love you, and if you'll give me one more chance, I'll do everything I can to make this right. Counseling, take it slow, whatever you want."

"I can't think beyond trying to stay alive right now."

A noisy exhalation through pursed lips gave away his disappointment. He took the smart option; he nodded and shut up. We hastened to catch up with Micah and Simon, who'd stopped and was pointing to a flickering light about fifty feet in front of us.

It was even stranger than before. The houses were there, then not, then there again. They were fading in and out with the rhythm of the light. We all turned off our flashlights and huddled in a tight circle. "Okay, this was a bad idea from the start but now what do we do?" I whispered. "If we can only see the houses for a few seconds, how are we ever gonna get in? And does anyone recognize which one we were in the last time? Because they all look the same to me."

"Also, we thought one of the houses had lights on. But it isn't from one house, now they're all lit up like it's Christmas." Micah huffed.

"I don't think it matters which one we go into. I know it sounds crazy, but I feel like those houses are a bridge," said Simon.

"Too what?" My eyes widened.

"To wherever the creature came from."

Gideon interjected, "I know this is gonna sound wild but hear me out. It's something I've thought about ever since we connected your sighting with mine. The more I look at this neighborhood, the more it makes sense to me," he continued. "The way we were being watched at the casino, the whole thing with Simon and Catherine being separated from their group. What if it's some kind of experiment? People are brought here. They must brainwash them or do something to erase their memories. Like your wife, you said she couldn't remember where she'd been, and neither could you. And if the town isn't visible to anyone, no harm, no foul. Whatever their grand plan, you must have caught a glitch, enabling you to see this neighborhood from the hotel window.

"Who's they?" I pleaded.

"That's what we have to find out." Gideon looked over his shoulder at the stage show. "Let's just pick one."

"I think we should all turn back now and drive home. Maybe we can convince someone to listen to us when we get there. And *they* can come and check this out. Simon, I know you're in agony, and for that, I'm truly sorry. But getting yourself killed is not going to bring Catherine back." It sounded reasonable to me.

"Jessie is right," said Simon. "You should all go back. I knew from the start this was a bad idea. If something happens to me, then so be it. I'm responsible for myself. But taking all of you with me is insane and not something Catherine would have wanted me to do. I'm going in on my own, and you are all heading home. Now."

Okay good. Simon was the voice of logic, and then Micah chimed in, "I agree with Gideon." When the hell did she get so heroic? "I still think we need evidence. If we go to the police, even in a group, what are we gonna say? Anything we tell the cops is gonna sound like we partied too hard. Even Simon, especially Simon. He just lost his wife, his grief is overwhelming, and for all the police know, he could've taken anything to slay that beast."

I couldn't believe what I was hearing. Who was this person? All of a sudden, she's *Black Widow*?

"We're stronger together. If we do encounter more of those things, at least we'll have a fighting chance in numbers. If we go back, I think we're signing Simon's death certificate for sure, and I won't do it."

My heart pounded. "Micah. I get what you're saying. I do. But do you remember what happened the last time we came across that monster? Furniture moving on its own. Us being trapped in that room, windows and doors disappearing? Think. We were damn lucky last time to get out alive. We don't even know how many of them there are. We need to go back to Vegas, all of us." I thought I had made a pretty decent argument. Any logical person like Micah would have to agree.

"I'm staying with Simon." Great. She wasn't leaving him, and I certainly wasn't leaving her. Back to where we started. Finally, we decided that Simon would scout ahead. If things looked okay, he would beckon the rest of us.

"It would be better if we entered the same model house because at least we had some idea of where to go once inside," Gideon commented.

"How are we supposed to do that? We have no way of

knowing the floorplan. What if each one is different? What if they lead us nowhere? Simon's theory is built on shaky ground."

I bit the inside of my cheek, a calming method that was painfully dumb.

Simon crept around the camouflage of dry sage, barrel cactus, and marigolds. About fifteen feet in, he motioned for us to join him. Micah was looking away in the distance and didn't notice his signal. I nudged her arm, but instead of falling into step, she grabbed me and pointed to the row of houses. "Watch," she whispered.

I gasped in horror. A crowd of people, maybe twenty of them, were being led into one of the homes by an ogre-sized man in a dark suit. It was hard to see their features, but their shuffling feet and straight forward stare suggested a semi-conscious state as they filed in one by one.

I spun around looking for Gideon, but he'd already joined Simon, and both of them were focused on us and not the action going on right behind them.

"Crap on a cracker, they're not even seeing this."

Micah rolled her eyes.

We ran to the guys, ducking low and staying close to whatever brush was along the way. When we reached them, I grabbed Gideon and crouched down.

"Look." I pointed.

Micah had come up alongside me. "I think it's pretty obvious that's the one we start with."

"Okay. We'll wait a few minutes until they've all gone inside. If he's taking them to that surgical room, they could be doing anything. Experiments, taking a walk through that weird wall, we don't know. It's better if I go in alone first, less noise," said Gideon.

"No mate, this one's on me. I'll go in."

"Listen before anyone goes anywhere, what do you think you're gonna find?" I asked Simon.

"Do you remember that strange mark I told you about? The one Catherine had on her hip? It was unlike anything I'd ever seen before."

"Yeah, I get it, you said it was strange." I glanced back at the house. A few more deadheads were being led in.

"What I didn't tell you was it resembled a tattoo, but the bloody thing was completely healed. It looked as if she'd had it for years. She might not have even noticed it if it weren't so tender."

"What could've done that?"

Simon looked to the stars.

My head felt foggy, like I'd just woken up from a night of Benadryl and Vegas allergies. "I'm not following."

"I think maybe there's more portals than just the one that accesses the desert. They have to come from somewhere."

"Wait. Are you saying you think they're coming from another planet?"

"I don't know. Yes. Maybe. I'm not sure. It's all bloody confusing."

"Wow." Micah took in three deep breaths. "I mean, it makes sense, right?"

"Sure. If we're in a Stephen King novel." I pulled my hair back and twisted it into a make-shift bun. "I don't know ... maybe."

"Let's just go see what we find." Gideon nodded in the direction of the house. "The doors shut, now's your chance, Simon."

I held my breath as Simon scurried from one sagebrush to the other until he was close enough to scamper to the door.

"This is grueling." I rubbed my forehead.

Slowly, he turned the knob. It was open. He slipped through, disappearing from our sight.

The acid in my stomach roiled, swishing its way to the back of my throat. I swallowed to extinguish the burn. I was worried about our new friend, and when the door opened, and Simon stepped out waving us on, my nerves calmed to a tolerable level.

Into the house of horrors we go.

CHAPTER 8
ALIENS

IT WAS DARK INSIDE, but with our flashlights, we could see the room was a duplicate of the previous one.

"I think we should go upstairs," suggested Gideon.

"Yeah, maybe there's another peculiar attic." I chimed in.

The six of us cat-walked through the room. I grabbed Micah's arm and leaned in to whisper. "Okay, I know it's a little late for this, but what are we going to do once we find the entry? I might have missed something, but the way I see it, no one has a plan." Micah shrugged. Great.

We found the staircase to the rear of the home, off the kitchen. Different than the last house we had been in. Toe to heel, we tightened the space between us and climbed the stairs. The hairs on the back of my neck stood at attention as I kept looking behind me for Mr. Wizard. A cuter name than the monster deserved, but it eased the tension in my already horrified brain.

At the top of the stairs were a long hallway and several doors. I felt a little like a contestant in a bizarre game show. Behind door number one is death and dismemberment, door number two, a trip to a nifty little planet of mind-melting monsters. Take your pick.

"I think we should start the search with the room at the end of the hallway and work our way back," suggested Simon.

"Death and dismemberment it is," I muttered.

"What?" Micah whispered.

"Never mind. Sounds like a plan. Lead the way."

Approaching the door, I felt my stomach churn. I'd secretly hoped all the doors were locked. An impenetrable force that would leave us no choice but to abandon this stupid idea and go home. Simon slowly turned the crystal knob, the door opened with ease. Damn.

Inside, Gideon spotted a door to the crawl space. There was a picture window on the opposite wall, and I walked over to look out. This time it didn't disappear, but I saw no lights from the strip, mountain silhouettes, or even the stars, for that matter—nothing. It was as if I was looking into the mouth of a black hole.

"Micah. Come over here and check this out."

"We're in the middle of the desert. I don't think that's too unusual."

"No. I can't see *anything*. No mountains, stars, lights."

Micah pressed her face up to the glass and sighed, "It's just more weirdness."

I guess that pretty much summed it up. Nothing would surprise us anymore.

Gideon had gotten the vent cover opened and jumped up. Extending his hand, Micah and I followed one by one with Simon at the rear.

This time, there was a soft glow from a standing lamp, not total darkness. I felt a small sense of relief.

The room was different. There were no instruments or medical equipment, it was just a *room*. A large brass bed and dark mahogany dresser reminded me of the early 1900s. Beside the bed, a tall mirror, framed with the same cherrywood, proudly nestled in the corner. On the opposite wall, a low dressing table displayed a silver brush, comb, and mirror trimmed in Dresden Rose. My heart skipped a beat. I recognized the pattern immediately. My great-grandmother had a nearly duplicate set that she let me play with as a child.

Standing in the center of the room, we pivoted around. I caught Micah, her eyes wide with confusion. All I could do was shake my head. I'm not sure exactly what all of us expected to see, but this didn't even come into the realm of possibilities. It all looked so normal—for 1910, that is.

Gideon began pressing gently against one of the walls to check for a hidden passageway, and the rest of us did the same. It was Simon who found it. His hand just passed through like it was water. He gasped, and we clamored around him. We were standing so close I doubt you could have wedged a piece of paper between either one of us.

Beads of sweat were dripping off his forehead, falling like raindrops on his white Nike's. He was scared. So was I. The sharp pain in my chest as my heart pressed against my rib cage was a constant reminder it could be my last breath.

Fully submerged up to his wrist, a part of Simon had crossed the divide between us and whatever was on the other side. I grabbed his forearm and slowly pulled until his hand was completely visible again.

"Let me try." Gideon stepped up to the wall.

"Wait, mate, let's go together."

I clung to Gideon's belt loop, and the faintest of smiles touched his eyes. I let my fingers fall away, breaking his tether to our world. Sentiment silenced behind sealed lips, I watched them slip away.

When they were about halfway submerged, the back of their heads, torso, and legs reminded me of an exhibit I'd seen back in Las Vegas. Real human cadavers sliced in half and on display. When they finally disappeared, I found myself shuffling from one end of the wall to the other. My fingers tapping along the side of my jeans sounded oddly like the theme song from *Friends*.

My nervous serenade was abruptly interrupted as the boys stepped back into our reality. I quickly scanned them, making sure everything was intact. Arms, legs, hands, feet—it was all there.

Simon leaned against Micah and then slid down to the floor. Gideon swayed from side to side before sitting down.

"We found something," Simon said after a few deep breaths. "It looks like we picked the right place because we're pretty sure the answers we're looking for are on the other side of that wall."

My stomach plummeted. I knew this was what we were searching for, but now it was all too real.

"It enters a neighborhood very much like this one. At first glance from the window, we could see other houses, driveways, cars, streetlights. But when we looked past all that—it wasn't our world."

Blowing a lock off her brow, Micah asked, "What did you see?"

"It would be easier to show you. Give me your hand."

Micah instinctively withdrew and then, reconsidering, hesitantly placed her trembling hand in Simon's. Gideon gently locked his fingers around mine, and I tightened my grip. Gingerly we took the first step.

My eyes squeezed shut; I tottered through the unknown. I could hear Micah mumbling frantically in front of me. The temperature dropped thirty degrees. I shivered uncontrollably, and Gideon clutched my hand a little tighter.

"It'll be over in a sec," he whispered.

I managed to squeak out, "Okay."

"You can open them now."

Consumed with fear and excitement, I relaxed my lids, allowing them to drift open. The pale blue walls, trimmed with a border of cartoon race cars, suggested we were standing in a little boy's bedroom. The olive green and blue comforter on the twin-sized bed was folded back like an open gate ushering in the new day after a serene slumber. The allure of toys spread out across the beige and gold Berber carpet tugged at the child inside me, but the room felt too familiar, and that made it very, very creepy. I brushed my hand along the goosebumps erupting on my arms. Facing the bed was a large window. Micah wouldn't take her eyes off the view.

"What do you see?"

"I think you better come over here."

I joined my BFF, and the guys fell in behind us.

"Crazy, right?" Gideon inched closer, his chest brushing across my back.

At first glance, everything seemed normal. But on further inspection of the horizon, I felt a little sick. The sky was a blinding reddish-orange, and as I pressed my face up to the glass to see more, I caught a glimpse of two suns. I pulled back quickly—the glass was hot. I live in Las Vegas, where some days the temperature can rise past a hundred and ten, but this felt *much* warmer.

"There are two suns. Where the hell are we?" My pulse throbbed in my temples. "You guys, is it just me, or is anyone else thinking about what happens if we can't get back home?"

I glanced over at Gideon and rolled my eyes. The jackass was taking a photo of the sky.

"What? It's cool." Gideon slipped the phone into his pocket.

"Let's not get ahead of ourselves. I think we should do some investigating first. Maybe check out the block and surrounding area." Simon eyed the three of us like he was waiting for approval.

"No one separates from the group, got it?" Gideon

sounded like the obvious hero in a slasher flick who *really* isn't the hero.

I didn't need anyone telling me not to stray; the heavy weight of trepidation was enough to keep me from wandering.

The first floor of the house had a contemporary design. A tan microfiber couch butted up to one wall in the living room, facing a large TV complete with cable box and game system. The dining room table was a light wood with seating for six and a picture of the desert night hung perfectly centered on the wall—a typical Las Vegas home smack dab on an alien planet.

Gideon was the first to reach the front door. He slowly turned the knob and cracked it open. He peered from side to side, then waved for us to follow. We all stepped out to the front porch and stayed close.

The reddish-orange sky was blinding, and the atmosphere felt like the inside of an oven. The oxygen filled our lungs with the weight of two 5lb barbells and breathing was much more difficult than what we were used to.

"It must be a hundred and twenty," I panted. "How the hell are we going to move around when we can barely breathe?"

Gideon grabbed my hand. "We'll just have to take our time and move slowly. Don't talk much, and we'll be okay."

"Yeah, but we don't even know if what we're breathing in can hurt us." The conversation alone was leaving me exhausted.

"Jess, we're here. Let's just nose around and see if we can't figure out what the frig is going on."

If I had the energy, I'd wallop him in the head.

"Jess may be right." Micah was my savior. "We have no clue if this atmosphere is dangerous. It could slowly be killing us. Simon, I want to help you, but what if she's right?"

"Like I said before, none of you should have to do this

with me," Simon spoke softly. "But I have to. I owe it to Catherine, and we need to find out exactly what's going on. You and Jess go back to the house. I'll keep on, and Gideon, whatever you choose to do, no worries."

Gideon looked at me and then again at Simon. *Uh oh...he's going.*

"I don't think separating is such a hot idea. As for dying, the atmosphere feels a little heavier, but I think our bodies will adjust."

Ugh. I hate logic sometimes.

Micah crossed her arms. "Okay. We stay together."

Swiping his forehead with the back of his arm, he squinted. "I think we need to follow the street and see where it leads. This neighborhood is set up to look like Las Vegas. I want to know where we really are." We all nodded and then blindly followed. As much as I wanted a plan or some sort of shred of knowledge that we had the slightest idea that we knew what we were doing, we didn't.

Nearing the end of the block, I felt like Dorothy in *The Wizard of Oz*. Except that, instead of cute little munchkins and beautiful technicolor, the color was fading. Trees and bushes that were green a few moments ago began to lose all their luster, slowly fading away to the dull replacement of black and grey. The further from the houses we got, the more forested the scenery became, thick with the void of color. *What the hell is this place?* My brain was on overload.

We trudged past thick, full timbers, each one duller than the next. It was so weird. Growing up in the desert, you get used to the lack of lush greenery. But even the most desert-adapted plants have some color, even if it's faded and muted. This was like looking at a pencil rendition of a forest.

We had been following Gideon for about half an hour when he stopped dead in his tracks. Simon came up behind him and halted too. I wasn't sure if I wanted to move forward or not, but curiosity took over, and I joined them with Micah in tow.

There, maybe about a ten-minute walk away, was a city. The buildings didn't look anything like those we were used to seeing in Vegas, or anywhere for that matter. Most of them were extremely tall and silver—not mirrored or reflective, but like brushed stainless steel. There were no visible windows, and they blended in with the grey and black of the surrounding trees. It was as if they had taken their design cue from the foliage.

"Crap, it's boiling out here. Simon, can I have a water, please?"

He reached into his backpack, the smile on his face came crashing down. "I don't think you want this. It's really hot."

"Damn, we need to get some water."

"What if they don't have water?" Micah raised a brow.

"Right now, as long as it's wet and cold, I'm in."

Thoughts of cool water teased my parched throat, and I swished what little saliva I could create around the inside of my mouth. We stayed close to the tree line; the enormous, low-hanging branches of a species I couldn't begin to recognize worked nicely to shield most of our movement. The large, steel grey leaves reminded me a little of my dad's fig tree, only on steroids. Choosing an even, brisk gate, we'd travel several feet, stop, assess our surroundings, and then move on.

When we reached the city limits, a river of sour liquid gushed to the back of my throat. I swallowed hard and winced. My hands and feet tingled, and breathing grew more difficult. Micah must have recognized the growing panic on my face because she grabbed my hand and squeezed it very tightly. She pulled me closer to her.

"You're okay, just a little panic attack. Take some deep breaths."

"Guys, we need a break."

She walked me over to one of the last full trees before the pavement, and we sat under a canopy of pointed, black needles. If I wasn't completely unhinged, I might have appreciated the beauty of an onyx pine tree but given my pseudo brush with death...not so much. I'd never had that feeling before, and I hope I never do again.

My BFF continued to soothe me, calling to mind goofy things we did in our childhood, and with a few more deep breaths, my calm had returned. We rested for as long as it took me to get through a chorus of Lady Gaga's *Paparazzi* in my head before moving on.

We reached the first building, and Gideon peered around the corner. Simon moved behind him.

"Do you see anything?" I kept my voice to a whisper.

"No, it's pretty quiet." Gideon kept his eyes on the view. Click.

"Really? Put the fucking phone away."

I squeezed between the guys to get a better look. It took all my strength not to punch Gideon in the face.

Whoever inhabited this world really loved silver. Plunked along the sidewalk, maybe every twenty feet, were four-foot-high cubes made from the same material as the buildings. There must be dozens because they stretched along the city block as far as the eye could see.

"Look at those things." I pointed. "What are they, some kind of art?"

In Vegas, the city started an art project to beautify the addition of highways and storefronts. They hired local artists to create sculptures that reflected the desert wildlife. I thought maybe this was similar.

"No, I think they're more than that. Check out that tube-like thing on the side of it." Gideon observed.

"That could be cup dispensers, maybe there's water. I mean, it is like a million degrees." Micah fanned her face.

"I'll go check it out." Gideon took a step, but Simon grabbed his arm.

"Not so quick, mate. You're all here because of me. I'll go."

"Wait ..." Simon left before Gideon could utter another word. Keeping in line with the buildings, he scurried along the sidewalk until he reached the box. Leaning from side to side, he inspected the object before he reached his hand out and waved it over a hole the size of a silver dollar in the front panel. Out came a clear liquid. He reached for a cup from the dispenser and filled it. He rested his back against the building and smelled the cup, then dipped a finger in and placed it in his mouth. He smiled and gave us a thumbs up. Whew. I finally let out the breath I didn't know I was holding.

We scurried to the silver oasis, staying close to the buildings. My hair matted to the sides of my face, and I tucked the drenched strands behind my ears before swiping my hands on the bottom of my camisole.

Simon poured each of us a cup of the life-sustaining liquid, and we drank as if we'd been stuck in the Mojave for days. The cold was soothing on my dry throat, and it had a bit of an earthy taste, like the water from the end of a garden hose.

The suns began their descent behind the horizon, their illuminating beauty conflicting with the ashen terrain below. We decided to wait until dark before venturing further into the city.

A portrait of stars painted across the darkening sky as the buildings fell into shadows. The solid façade transitioned as lights abruptly switched on in the buildings, unmasking windows to the interior.

We cautiously started our migration further into the mystery. A storefront materialized in front of me, black and grey metal signs hung in the dusty windows advertising ice-cold jugs of water for $1 and other items I didn't recognize.

Across the street, a restaurant with a half-lit neon sign blinked —*Open*. A handwritten cardboard sign above the door stated no walk-ins. I looked around the desolate street and shrugged; no worries there.

"Hey," I whispered. "Does anyone else find it odd that we're in a strange world and everything from the signs to the prices are posted in English?"

"At this point, Jess, everything is odd so why not?" Micah swiped a bead of sweat off her top lip.

"Point taken."

We hadn't gotten very far when we noticed a flurry of *people* emerging from the far end of the city. Aside from their monotone choice in fashion, you wouldn't know they weren't human. Crowding in like opening day at the county fair, couples walked hand in hand, women in small groups laughed like besties, and families with their children running ahead as their parents cautioned them to wait, brought life into what was a ghost town just minutes ago. We huddled under the alcove of an unlit drug store before we realized no one was paying any attention to us.

Simon pointed to a small alley between two of the buildings, and we followed him.

"Anyone else think it's strange that not one of them even gave us a second look?" Simon nervously scanned the area.

"Extremely weird. But what's got me is, I was expecting something more like that thing we saw in the desert. These people look like—*people*." I sighed.

"That jarred me too," said Micah.

I peeked around the edge of the building. Something felt familiar about these people; I just couldn't...oh, wait, that's what it is. The way they moved, so slowly, reminded me of the waitress at the café, the bartender, and the goons standing guard at the casino doors. Even Smith walked like he was trudging through mud.

"You know, these people here walk a lot like the staff back at the casino and hotel. Their movement is slow and exaggerated, like they're all exhausted. I thought maybe the staff was just being forced to help Smith and his goons. Maybe under some kind of mind control or something. But what if they *are* them? It would make perfect sense. Smith would have total control over everything as the hotel and casino manager. And why not do it themselves? They blend in just like anyone else."

"But the kids are running around, and the cliques of friends seem energetic." Gideon ran his fingers through his hair. "That doesn't track with your theory."

"Maybe it happens after a certain age? And I didn't say they were exhausted; I said they walked like they were. Maybe their movement is a reflection of this place. As they get older, the heat, the life, slow their reflexes. That would explain the children running and playing."

Gideon raised a brow like he was mulling over the possibilities.

But I was really creeped out. If a whole town in Nevada was alien and no one knew it, how many other towns could be affected? Until now, I had assumed we only had to worry about Primm. What if the entire world was populated already? I just wanted to go back two days and be ignorant again. How could we do anything if we can't even distinguish them from us?

"Jess, there's another thing. Look how all of them are wearing black and grey. Just like the buildings, trees, plants, it's all only those two shades—no color." Micah took a quick peek at what was now a bustling city. "Smith, all he wore was a black suit. And the hulks guarding the door, black suits. The waitress, a grey dress."

"This is impossible." I knew I sounded bitchy.

"No, this could be a good thing," said Gideon. "If we can

get some other clothing, we might be able to blend in. We'd have a better shot of finding some answers."

"That's a good idea," I spoke up. "But right now, all we need is for one of us to blend in. If there's only one person moving around, chances are they won't notice. If we move in a herd, we'll be obvious. I think we can piece together one outfit that will work. Hopefully, that'll be good enough for one of us to go looking for clothes. We just need to decide which one of us will be going."

After several minutes of arguing our cases for heroism, Simon won out. Only because the guys had a mash-up of grey and black in their ensembles, and Micah and I had gone with warm shades of Summer.

Simon's jeans were black, and I had him switch shirts and tennis shoes with Gideon, who had been wearing a black T-shirt and grey Nikes. When Simon was done dressing, Micah's keen eye for fashion gave him the once over. "I think this will work." She stepped back and smiled.

Whispering good luck to our new friend, the rest of us hunkered behind the building, watching Simon assimilate into the alien culture. That's the second time I allowed my mind to form the word, but I guess we were really the aliens in this world. My palms started to sweat. My stomach felt like a waging war, and I was about to be the loser.

I looked over at Micah. Her face had a green hue.

She was really becoming attached to Simon, kind of like the lost puppies she'd rescued over the years. Micah had a knack for finding strays in need, whether animal or human; her heart was as big as they come.

She inched closer to me and grabbed my hand. I could feel the tension in her body. I gave her a smile. And then, despite my own lack of conviction, I told her he would be okay. To be honest, I wasn't sure if he would be safe, but it did make her relax a little.

Simon slowly disappeared out of view as he made his way further into the city. By now, people were everywhere. It reminded me of the time I'd been to Manhattan at midday. It was full of excitement and energy, and this city felt similar. Only they came out after dark, avoiding the heat of two suns.

Sitting and waiting was the worst. At least if we were moving, we weren't easy targets. Micah was uncharacteristically quiet, and Gideon was tapping his hand repeatedly on his leg. It sounded like a huge drum nestled right up against my ear. Deafening.

"Gideon. Quit it. You're driving me nuts. We're supposed to be inconspicuous. You trying to be a one-man band isn't great for our cover."

"Sorry, I just feel like I should be doing *something*. This is driving me crazy."

"Yeah, well, join the club. I think all of us feel a little crazed right now."

I soaked in the shadows of a world that was not our own. Primm felt so far away, like a dream I had once. It's strange how your mind can do that.

CHAPTER 9
WHERE'S SIMON

SIMON CONTINUED DOWN the long city block, peeking into store windows and looking over his shoulder. A pale green glow illuminating from above stole my attention from our new friend. The streetlights had switched on, casting an eerie glow on the alien town.

Simon crossed the street and stopped in front of a closed hat shop. He bent down and pretended to tie his shoe, casually looking up. No one gave him the slightest hint of recognition. Trailing my vision from Simon to the clothing store, I observed several customers taking items off the racks and bringing them inside. He slipped in after them, and we waited. After ten grueling minutes, he emerged with a few pairs of pants and some shirts thrown over his arm. He looked about as inconspicuous as a deranged killer clown. Gideon inched out from behind the side of the building, and Micah peered over his shoulder. Simon partially raised his arm and smiled, but it quickly faded.

A pulsing nee-nore, nee-nore, resonated from the roof of several black Hummers barreling down the street from the opposite end of town, stopping in front of Simon, creating a barricade between him and everything else. He dropped to his knees, the blood draining from his face.

"By order of the true commander, we place you under arrest, thief."

The baritone directive echoed over the din of the siren as my pulse throbbed in my temples, blurring my vision. I desperately rubbed my eyes, trying to clear the haze. Micah covered her ears and dropped to the ground. Gideon pushed her back out of sight.

Five very large men dressed in dark grey from head to toe quickly surrounded Simon. The men wore helmets with shields, completely concealing their faces. They grabbed him with such force that it knocked him to the ground. One of them took out something similar to a nightstick. Radiating a green glow as he ran it alongside our friend's body, Simon's legs and arms grew rigid as he remained motionless and levitated from the ground, hovering in midair.

A cry stuck in the back of my throat.

The head-exploding shrill ceased, and my eyes began to clear. I struggled for breath seeing poor Simon's plight. His head was turned toward us, eyes fixed and wide. Gideon took a step forward but halted when Micah being *Micah*, scrambled to her feet and attempted a one-woman rescue. Gideon caught her just in time. He pulled her back, whipping them both around, and knocking them against the side of the building.

"We need to follow them ... together."

Micah's shoulders dropped, and her eyes softened. She wiped a tear from her cheek. "You're right."

We observed, powerless, as Simon's body floated into the open end of one of the vehicles.

"Crap—how do we follow them in that?" My voice cracked a little.

"We'll stick close to the buildings. They're in traffic, so

they shouldn't be moving that quickly. Hopefully, they won't travel out of the city," said Gideon.

The vehicle was on the move—taking Simon with it.

We were risking exposure, but we followed the black Hummer diligently, staying as close to the buildings as possible. Weaving through the hordes of night owls, no one noticed us or maybe didn't care who we were. I tried to catch a glance from several of the shoppers passing by, but there was no reaction. Not a glare, not a word.

I did catch a whiff of garlic wafting from a small shop with a long, grey wooden sign hanging from two chains. The black letters simply read ... Bread. Normally the aroma of one of my favorite flavors permeating from dough rising would draw me in, but the potent tang coming from an alien baker just added to the sour feeling in my gut.

Fortunately for us, there were several stoplights, and the vehicle caught every one of them. With each stop, we clamored to the nearest retail, trying to appear like we were shopping and hoping our clothing didn't get us noticed.

Micah was the first to state the obvious. "Don't you think this is sort of crazy? I mean, we stick out like a sore thumb. I mean—really? It's not like they can't see us."

My wheels had been turning ever since the police showed up. Simon wore the same colors as everyone else, and yet, they caught him. We're walking around amongst them, and not so much as a side-eye has come our way.

"I think I figured it out," I said with a hint of pride.

"Figured what?" Micah blinked.

"I know why they haven't noticed us—it's because they can't. Look at what they're wearing and the surroundings. There's no color."

"So poor Simon got caught for nothing." Frustration rang thick in Micah's voice.

"Not for nothing. Now we know we can move around relatively unnoticed."

We continued following the car that had our friend. It was so strange, we had only known Simon a short time, but it felt like years. He fit into our group as if he had been with us all along. Now that he was in danger, it was killing us. We had to get him back, no matter what.

My theory proved itself with each person we skated by that held no interest in us. I accidentally grazed a woman as I walked too close, and she looked around as if a light breeze had tickled her arm. The invisible factor was cool but also disturbing.

The car turned into a driveway that led to a large black building. High black iron gates blocked the front entrance. Opening like ominous wings, they welcomed the three-ton vehicles across the threshold to whatever resided in 123 Creep Street.

We tried to make it through, but they closed before we could get there. We stood and watched as the Hummer seemed to be swallowed up by the winding road that led to the big black box.

Gideon motioned for us to come closer.

"I'm going to go around the property and see if there's another way for us to get in," he said. "You wait here."

"You've got to be kidding me," I snapped. "Really? I'm the one who figured out the color thing and the fact that Primm is alien. You can go check to the left side; Micah and I will go right."

He looked down at the ground and nodded. "Okay."

He walked around the left side of the building while Micah and I used the cover of sculpted hedges to follow along the property on the right.

A plethora of hedges and more fencing squashed my hope

that we'd find a way in, as did the security cameras hanging from the eaves.

We returned to the front of the property, but Gideon wasn't there. I sat on a large boulder that butted up to the fence. Micah sat beside me. Crevices in the stone were bumpy under my bum, and I wiggled to find a flat spot.

"Hey, I think I know how we can climb over." I patted the rock.

"Oh, brilliant."

Standing on the boulder, I jumped up and reached for the top of the bars. Once I had a grip, I climbed up the iron using the toe of my sneakers until I was sitting on top of the fence with one leg thrown over the other side. I was getting ready to jump when Gideon rounded the corner of the property and waved for us to follow him.

Bummed over the interruption to my mild victory, I jumped down next to Micah, and the two of us made a left turn.

"I found a way in on the far side of the fence," he said. "There's a smaller gate, and it's not locked. I almost missed it because it was covered with some bushes. We can get in, and after that, we'll figure it out."

Gotta love the details in Gideon's plan.

We followed him to the open gate, and one by one, walked through. There had to be two miles between us and the front door. Even though no one had noticed us so far, we kept to the cover of the topiary. On each side of us were thick, smokey grey trees and raven-black bushes, some taller than the house. A pathway led to a front door, so pristine it could have been cut from granite, lined in perfectly manicured grey hedges. Not one leaf or branch was out of place.

Slinking around the property, I took note of how beautiful our surroundings were. There was a surprisingly calm, serene feeling being in the center of such monochromatic perfection.

The night was much cooler than the swelter of the day, and the city lights glimmered and twinkled in the landscape. It almost felt magical. That is until I remembered we were all in grave danger and could end up becoming part of the very landscape I had been admiring. From the corner of my eye, I noticed something run across the tree line about ten feet away from us. Narrowing my eyes, I studied the shadows. A small, dark, and light grey speckled creature emerged. It was about the size of a rabbit and with a similar body, but this guy had no fur. The textured bumps of his skin resembled a reptile more than a mammal. Hopping like a bunny, he paused when he noticed me staring. Locking his glowing amber eyes on me, he quickly scurried under the brush of low-hanging pine trees.

"Jess. Jess!"

Gideon used his pointer finger to beckon me. We crept along the back side until we were facing a back door.

"Jessie, get the hell over here." As I slipped by him through the door, he gave me that *what were you thinking* look. I decided now wasn't the time for sarcastic comebacks and just kept walking. Inside, Micah felt around for a switch on the wall. She was about to flip it when I grabbed her hand.

"No. We don't want to attract any attention. We have no idea where we are or how close they are. Let's just give our eyes a second to adjust. We should be able to get around fine with the light shining in from outside." She nodded.

After a moment or two, the shadows began to clear. We were in what appeared to be a kitchen. Not the kind of kitchen you'd see your mom cooking a Thanksgiving turkey in — more like the inner workings of a fine restaurant, with big convection ovens and more stainless steel than I have ever seen. An industrial-size sink was surrounded by large mixing bowls, next to a freestanding contraption I guessed was some sort of mixer.

The room was so large that you could probably entertain twenty-five or thirty people in it—my Italian grandmother's dream.

We whisked past the sea of stainless steel through a large threshold leading to a long, unusually wide hallway. Black doors spaced about five feet part hung like framed artwork against the pale grey walls. Dark grey tables, topped with black, grey, and white floral arrangements accented the corridor.

Me and Gideon listened at each door, advancing with caution while Micah kept an eye out behind us. The house was so huge that finding Simon was a daunting task, but there was no way we were giving up.

Losing patience, I decided to let Gideon finish the door to door while I continued to the end of the hall. A black and white portrait of the city framed in etched silver hung over a small table against the wall. I brushed past them and found myself standing at the top of a long, winding staircase. The room below was dark, and the visibility on the stairs was limited at best.

I had no idea what lay below, but I had my foot on the first step when Micah pulled me back. I don't know why, but I would have continued if she hadn't stopped me. Micah looked at me as if I had lost my mind.

"Are you crazy, Jess? What the hell were you thinking, going ahead of us like that?" She was pissed.

"I don't know. I just couldn't stop myself. Maybe it was the hallway—it felt too confining."

"Confining? This frigging hallway must be a mile wide. What is going on with you?" She knitted her brow.

"Nothing. I just thought—no, correct that, I *wasn't* thinking. I just kept going, that's all."

She gave me that look that only Micah can give, the one that confirms you're an idiot with just a narrowing of her eyes. And it doesn't stop there. Somehow, she keeps the intense stare for what feels like forever while her mouth pulls into a strained frown. Words weren't needed. I always wind up feeling like a complete moron. It works every time.

"I'm sorry." She grabbed my arm and yanked me forward.

Gideon pushed by us and put his finger to his mouth. A faint moan hummed through the open staircase. After a few moments, we concluded it was just the air circulating to whatever hell those stairs lead to. The last door Gideon jiggled was unlocked. "I'll go in."

"Gideon," I hissed. "Let's just stay together no matter what goes down. We're stronger as a group." I gave him the you-know-deep down-inside-I still-love-you-and-don't want-anything-to- happen-to-you look. He nodded, raised my hand to his lips, and kissed it gently. Then he reluctantly let go and turned the knob.

CHAPTER 10

THE ROOMS

INSIDE, a large rectangular room divided into several smaller areas by thick, black rope mesmerized me. Each section was uniquely decorated as bedrooms, living rooms, and kitchens, from a different time in our history. Like a museum, except there weren't any guides, security guards, or paying guests—just us.

"I know I said stay together, but maybe we should each take an area and check it out. We'll save time. I'll search the one over there." I pointed to a 1950s mid-modern display.

Gideon clicked his way to the '70s, recording future Instagram posts.

Micah took the nineteenth century. Her sights set on the master bedroom stuffed with heavy, dark wood furniture, a King-sized brass bed, and floral tapestries. One of the hand-carved bureaus was so large, I bet it would take two to three husky men to move it.

I poked around my vintage family room, stopping in awe when I came to the RCA Victor standup model TV set. My great-grandma had one when I was about five—she wouldn't part with it. I looked around for Micah, I wanted to share my treasure, but I didn't see her. I assumed she was hidden by a sea of Mahogany.

As I ran my fingers over the tweed, olive sofa, a faint moan captured my attention. The hushed cry quickly grew to a loud and distinct plea for help—Micah. Rushing to the center of the room, Gideon joined me, and we frantically searched for her through a barrage of antiques and heavy furniture. Pushing pieces aside with my shoulder and body weight, I found her curled up on the side of a nightstand.

Her arms were wrapped around one of the legs of the four-poster bed. Her grip was so tight her knuckles had turned white.

What happened next could only be described as heart-stopping. She was *fading*, from a wavy blur back to her screaming self, and then waves again.

I reached out for the ghostlike apparition that was my BFF. Strands of hair stuck to her forehead, and tears streamed down her face. She was losing strength, and her screams dwindled to a whimper. I couldn't feel any more powerless.

"Gideon, help me!" I pleaded.

Both of us reached for a body part, any body part. He grabbed onto her legs, and I curled my fingers around hers. The three of us flashed in and out like some sort of Vegas magic show. I'm not sure where we went but judging by the flappers on stage and the red velvet seats filling the music hall, I'm guessing we had a front-row ticket to the 1920s.

After three passes to our vacation in time, I managed to get a grip on the nightstand, which had not been on this little journey of ours. Pulling my body closer, I was able to gain leverage enough to push me away from the portal bed. I still had a firm grip on the tail end of Micah's T-shirt.

"Gideon, let go of Micah and roll out of there. I've got her."

Gideon released his vice grip on her legs and rolled himself to safety. Once clear, he grabbed my torso and yanked, but Micah held onto the bedpost.

"Micah!" I shouted. "I've got you! Let go of the post."

My fingers started to go numb as she tightened her grip on the bed. Her gaze met mine, a flood of tears staining her cheeks. "I'm sorry," she said. "I can't."

As her body and the bed rippled away, Gideon yanked again, pulling me to freedom. My legs folded beneath me. I pressed my anger for Gideon into the triple dresser and used it as leverage to stand.

I waited for her return, but after several minutes of nothing, I realized she was gone.

"How could you do that?" My jaw tightened with disgust.

"It was one of you or none of you. Micah wasn't letting go."

"Then it should've been none." The words dripped from my lips like poison.

"I know you can't stand not knowing where she is, and you're pissed as hell at me, but Simon is somewhere in this house. If we find him, maybe we also uncover something that could help us with Micah. It's not what you want to hear, but I don't know what else we can do right now."

Finding Simon was the right thing to do; we really didn't have a choice. I clung to the hope that maybe Gideon was right. We left the room and crept down the winding staircase. It was so dark it was as if we'd been blindfolded. As the steps went deeper, my mind raced faster, and I thought about the last exchange I had with Micah. Her eyes had been filled with desperation and sorrow. If we don't find her...I pushed the thought out of my mind. There was no room for doubt; she was depending on me.

Gideon reached the bottom first, but just as I was about to step down and join him, we were assaulted by a very bright light. *What the hell?* All I could see was a white glare forming a halo around the shifting darkness. I closed my eyes and opened them slowly to adjust my vision.

We were completely surrounded by ten or twelve men, all dressed alike in dark grey shirts and black pants. Standing in the center was Jonathon Smith. My first instinct was to run back up the stairs, but something gave me the courage to stay. Or maybe it was stupidity.

Gideon charged Smith only to be restrained by four of the grey hulks. "Where the hell are our friends?" he shouted, pushing against them.

Smith calmly motioned for the others to let him go. He glided our way, his feet hovering several inches above the floor as if he were riding a cloud. Smith stopped in front of Gideon and lightly touched his forehead. Gideon erect, his head tilted downward.

"What did you do to him?" I leaned in so close Smith must have felt the rush of my breath.

"He's perfectly fine. There is no harm being done to him. I've merely put his brain to sleep for a moment to calm him."

"You put his brain to sleep? And you think that makes him perfectly fine? Stop whatever it is you're doing. Now." I stood inches away from Smith's face, his veins pulsating at his temples and his fists clenched tight. The anger he was holding back was about to break free. I'm not sure if the grey goons could sense this or if they were just being overly cautious, but they all moved closer to Smith. Smith held his hand up, and the group remained where they were. He paired intelligence with a cool exterior. I stood my ground. This creep stole my friends, put Gideon in a trance, and I was not about to show my fear to this bastard.

One of the goons placed his hand on Gideon's shoulder guiding him as they led us back up the stairs and into the first door on our left. Like a chosen audience member at Criss

Angel's Planet Hollywood show, Gideon remained in a hypnotic state.

The room had all the comforts of a normal sitting room, complete with couch, coffee table, and TV. An indifferent Smith approached Gideon and once again placed his hand on his forehead. Gideon raised his head and looked around the room. "Where are we?" He spun around, "Jess?"

I took his hand. "You okay?"

"A little dazed. How did we get here? I don't remember ..."

"Enough." Smith turned away.

I redirected my attention back to our captor. "Where's our friend Simon? We know you have him here somewhere, and we want him back. And while you're at it, tell us how we can get Micah. back, too."

"Micah?" Smith raised a brow. "I don't know anything about that. I'll admit, we do have your friend Simon, and he is completely fine. But as for your female companion, I have no idea where she is."

Gideon snapped. "Look, you piece of alien shit, cut the bull and give us our friends."

Smith kept his cool demeanor as he moved back and away from Gideon. With a motion of his hand, Smith's grey goons filed out of the room. I wasn't sure what was scarier, the fact that we were stranded in some strange world and our friends were missing, or that Smith really didn't need the protection of his goons.

"Alien?" he said smoothly. "You are on my planet. Here it's you who are the aliens. As for Micah, I've told you, I do not know where she is. She must be lost somewhere in the house."

"She's not in the house." I stepped forward.

"I am sorry, I do not understand. Did you lose track of her prior to reaching the house?"

"No. We lost her in one of the rooms."

"Ah, that is exactly what I said. She is somewhere in this house. We will locate—"

"No. She is not somewhere in this house. Micah is lost in one of those fucking rooms of yours. We were in what we thought was a bedroom. One of the rooms kept fading in and out, and Micah disappeared, along with everything from that room."

"It will be a bit time-consuming, but we will be able to retrieve her. We just need to know precisely which time she has traveled to. She is not lost, just misplaced for the moment."

I was ready to rip off Smith's head, but I bit the inside of my cheek instead. "If it helps, I think it's sometime in the 1920s."

"How do you know this?"

"Because we tried to save her, and in the process, we traveled with her."

"Yes. That does narrow it down."

"How do you plan on finding her?"

"It is difficult to explain, but we will."

"Try us." I stood firm, up close and personal in Smith's face. For the first time, Mr. Cool, Calm, and Strange-as-Hell showed a sign of emotion—frustration. His body tensed, and his lips tightened. Clearly, we were infringing on his day.

"Ahem." Smith cleared his throat. "We will track your friend with a time finder. It is a device we use to follow various time periods in your history. The room you saw her disappear in is logged. Each *bedroom,* as you referred to it, is recorded. We will find which room is missing and locate where, or, I should say, when she has found herself. Once we've done that, a team will retrieve her. It will take a while to review the recording and then proceed our sweep through time, but she will be perfectly fine until we bring her back. Your input has made it easier. Instead of centuries, we need only to look in a decade. "

"You don't know she's okay." I glared. "You have no idea what happened to her once she was stuck. I saw those people from the other time—they freaked. They don't know who or what Micah is. They could've done anything to her by now."

Smith crossed his arms.

I stopped, realizing I was wasting my breath. Smith was gonna do what he wanted, and I needed to keep my cool. There wasn't any reason to believe he was telling the truth, but right now, that's all we had to go on.

Apparently, Gideon didn't think the same way I did. He abruptly grabbed a nearby chair, swung it around his body, and used his momentum to crash it dead center into Smith's chest. Then followed it up with a swift kick to his legs, causing Smith to fall to the floor.

"What the fuck? He's our only lead to getting Micah back."

"I know, I just sort of snapped. He thought he held all the cards."

"Well, he kind of did."

I ran to the door and cautiously cracked it open. I saw no one. Behind me, Smith was slowly rising up from Gideon's surprise attack. We didn't wait around to see what he was capable of. The two of us were out the door in seconds running.

We skidded to a stop at the top of another descending staircase. Oh, great. Searching the unknown one dark, scary step at a time—again. We descended as quickly as possible without the guidance of any light. When we finally reached the bottom, we stayed close together. Thankfully, the windows bathed us in a soft, orange light from the emerging dawn. A faint conversation in the distance distracted me, and I caught Gideon's eye. He nodded to let me know he had heard it too.

Gideon stopped and whispered, "Look, there's a doorway about twenty feet to our right. I think we should check it out."

I agreed and followed him. At the door, Gideon pressed his ear to its smooth surface, then slowly turned the knob.

I felt like Charlie entering the Chocolate Factory for the first time. An Old-World study draped in hundreds of leather-bound books, some with gold leafing and gold embossed lettering, nestled on rows of deep, mahogany shelving. A rolling ladder to take your reading adventure to the next level —literally—stood waiting for its next enthusiast to glide across the treasure. I stepped lightly to avoid making noise, trailing my fingers along the tooled bindings as I passed. The rich aroma of leather enchanted me. What I would give to lie down in its buttery soft luxury.

An open novel rested atop a carved mahogany table next to an overstuffed herringbone chair. I lifted the book and scanned its pages. Not only did I not recognize the language, but I didn't even understand the letters—they were some sort of twisted hieroglyphics. I ran to a shelf and started flipping through book after book. Each one was as confusing as the first. I considered taking one, but the last thing we needed to do was make another enemy.

Daylight trickled through the window, bringing with it an intense heat. Outside the house, lights flickered out in each of the buildings as everything appeared to be closing. The grey goons were going to sleep.

I was exhausted. "What are we going to do? We're no closer to finding either one of them. Smith said they were going to locate Micah. Maybe we should have waited until we had her back before bolting."

"I don't trust him. Do you?" Gideon was leafing through one of the books.

"Well, no. But what choice did we really have?" I rubbed my temples, taking a deep breath and exhaling slowly.

"You see this?" Gideon held out the book.

"Yeah, they all have that weird writing."

"No, this one's different. Check this out." Gideon handed me the book. "It's in English."

On the cover were the words *The Journal of Tobias Johnson*. I opened the yellowed pages and carefully turned them from the corner. The writing had faded, but I was still able to read most of the entries.

September 29, 1863

They have taken my lovely Clarissa. Although I do not know where to search for her, I will not give up hope we might be reunited. They are not from this world, I fear. May God guide me through my quest.

I sat for a moment, soaking in the reality. These bastards have been at this for a long time. The more I read, the clearer it became that something sinister was happening back home.

I know now that I will only reunite with my beautiful Clarissa in our Lord's Kingdom. I fear I am fated to remain on this strange planet, with their two suns and a race that knows only darkness. They are a cunning and cruel people who are as devoid of emotions as their trees are of color. I know not if anyone will ever read these words, but the reader will be trapped as I. May the Lord see you through to the door back to our home.

I put the book down on the table. We both stood in somber reflection until I couldn't contain my thoughts any longer.

"I'm not sure what we thought was going to happen, but it's clear that if they had been coming to us all this time, whatever they wanted to do is not done. I mean, this journal is a hundred and sixty years old. What the hell?"

"We stick to the original plan. We find Simon and then look for Micah."

"I agree. I just don't think Smith has intentions of ever letting us leave. Call it a hunch, but you have to admit we know an awful lot about them now. They were counting on secrecy to execute whatever they're doing on our planet, but that'll be blown the minute we get away. Whatever their intentions are, they've taken great measures to execute them. Allowing us to return home would definitely ruin it for them. I trust nothing he says."

He nodded. "This shit just keeps getting deeper."

"I think we need to follow the voices we heard earlier and investigate them," I proposed. "I know it sounds crazy, but I think that's our best way of locating Simon. This house is huge, but maybe we'll be lucky enough to overhear information about him."

"Good idea." Gideon faintly smiled.

A golden beam illuminated tiny particles floating like fairies sprinkling pixie dust along the hallway. Like ninjas, we padded silently across the ebony wood floor. Through a partially opened door about ten feet down the hall, we heard voices, and the closer we got, the clearer they became. "Smith wants the one they call Simon to remain well. But he will grow weaker if he does not eat, they are a fragile species. I'll bring him some nourishment, and you wait here until I return. Then we will join in the hunt for the others."

This was the a-ha moment we had been waiting for. We just needed to follow the one with the groceries. Then Gideon motioned for us to go back down the hallway.

I took hold of his arm, and with a stabbing finger, I pointed to the door. He took my hand and silently pleaded for me to follow. When we were a distance away, Gideon spoke.

"Maybe we should split up," he whispered. "One of us follows the delivery guy, and the other one can stay here. We might find info on Micah if we track their conversation."

"Well, that's the dumbest thing you've ever said. We stay together. The last thing we need is to separate; then there'll be four of us lost in this monster house."

Gideon ran his fingers through his hair and sighed, "So we follow the dinner bell."

"Yup."

Down the hall, the door widened, and one of the grey goons sluggishly stepped into the hall. The two of us hid behind the curvature of the hallway, and when he was on the move, we scampered from doorway to doorway using the threshold as partial coverage. He slipped into the stairwell, and we waited a few seconds to allow enough space between him and us. I hadn't noticed until now, but Gideon had been right. Our movement and breathing had returned to normal—a small victory for us.

CHAPTER 11

WE FOUND HIM

EVERY ROOM WAS dimmer than the next. Given the intensity of their two suns, it made sense they were nocturnal.

"It feels like it's going to take days to search for Simon," murmured Gideon.

As we followed the goon down the stairs, I noticed a discrepancy.

"This building was extremely tall from the outside. Shouldn't there be more floors above us?"

"I've been thinking the same thing. And there aren't any stairs leading up. Let's see where this takes us. If we come up empty, we'll head back and look for an access to the floors above."

The next level down presented a new problem—the stairs split off into opposite directions, and we might have allowed the goon to get too far ahead. I could no longer hear the pinging of his shoes to metal.

"Which way do we go?"

Gideon pointed left. At this point, it was all just a crapshoot, so left we went.

Immediately I noticed the staircase was different from the others. It was constructed with a granite-like stone, rather than metal, with its steps worn in the center from the friction of countless travelers. A cool, damp residue darkened the surface, creating a medieval ambiance and possible slip hazard. Taking slow, hesitant steps, I couldn't decide what bothered me more, the thought of plummeting down solid stone or the icy chill numbing my fingers. The lower we descended, the colder it became, and I stopped for a moment to blow on my hands. I shivered uncontrollably, and Gideon reached from behind, running his hands up and down my arms to warm away the attacking goosebumps.

In the darkened passageway, we were just able to see the lighter clouds our warm breath made as it hit the frigid air. Continuing our descent, a buttery glow of light as we reached the bottom caught my eye. Following it, we turned a corner to a narrow hall. Numerous doors lined both sides, ending at a curved archway.

I heard a faint voice. "Did you hear that?" I asked.

"Yeah," he whispered.

"I'm really getting tired of opening doors," I muttered.

"I hear you, but I don't think we got a choice. We both heard something, shall we?" Gideon stretched his arm out in front of him, paving the way for our search. Methodically, we crept down the long hall, trying each knob unsuccessfully.

We were running out of doors when I noticed one of them was slightly ajar. Bright light spilled out, illuminating the threshold like heaven's gate.

I gravitated toward the door, my ears straining for any sound. A faint murmur slipped from behind the door.

Gideon whispered, "Ready?" I nodded, and we slowly pushed, inching the door open. My hands were clammy and slid across the splintered wood; droplets of blood smeared across my palm as my heart pounded. Air slowly escaped my lungs, and I struggled to take in a deep breath. In front of us, an oversized canopy bed crowned in dark grey, velvet drapes cascaded down four high posters, drawn closed. The carpet, a long-extinct tapestry print, reminded me of popular French decor from the 16th century. In fact, the whole room would've fit that time period very nicely.

"This lower level is different from the rest of the house. The entire basement looks like it was added after the home was built—it looks like medieval ruins. How the hell ..."

A fainthearted murmur interrupted Gideon—there was someone in the bed.

We softly stepped closer and hid behind the heavy drape of the canopy. Under a platinum black, silk coverlet, the frame of a man lying on his side faced the wall. His hair was dark brown like Simon's, but we couldn't see his face.

I eased closer to the man, who must be either sleeping or drugged because he didn't move. The stranger mumbled, and I recognized the accent—Simon. I yanked the covers off him, but he didn't respond.

"Something's wrong with him," said Gideon. "Simon!" he whispered sharply. "Simon!"

Simon strained to open his eyes.

"Come on, buddy, we need to get the hell out of here. Can you sit up?" Simon blinked without moving.

"Get up unless you're happy staying here with these damn —whatever they are," I commanded.

Gideon grabbed his arms and pulled him up until he was sitting on the edge of the bed. Simon rubbed his face and struggled to open his eyes. I tapped his cheek a few times, and Simon shook his head back and forth to force himself into consciousness.

"Gideon ... Jessie? Where are we?" His eyes straining to stay open, he gazed around the room. "Where's Micah?"

I looked away.

"Guys, where's Micah?" Simon was becoming more alert. He rubbed his palms on his knees.

"We don't know."

"What the bloody hell does that mean?"

"We lost Micah in another time."

"What are you talking about? Another time? What—"

"I'll explain everything, but we need to go, now."

Simon got up and began to stagger. Gideon put his arm around his waist to brace him, and I took hold of his left bicep.

We crept to the staircase like prisoners during a jailbreak, our eyes scanning the surroundings for an armed guard. Climbing the stairs back to the main floor took longer than the trip down because of Simon's weakened condition. We'd take a few steps and then rest, in between explaining to him everything he missed.

"Micah is bloody lost in some other time?" Simon repeated. "How the hell is that possible?"

"We haven't figured that out yet, but they're way more advanced than we are." I pressed my back against the wall. "Time travel, towns coming from nowhere—they've been doing this for a while. And by the way Smith spoke, they're not done yet."

Simon cleared his throat. "I don't know how we're gonna stop them, but we have to try."

After many twists and turns through darkened rooms, we ended up at our starting point—the library.

We eased him onto an overstuffed wingback chair.

"How you feeling? Any better?" I gazed out the window. The twin suns dawning over the horizon were a bleak reminder we were far from home.

The faintest of smiles touched his lips. "I'm okay. They really didn't do anything to this bloke. I spent most of the time in that room on the bed."

I felt calmer, a small consolation.

"Look." I handed him the journal of Tobias Johnson and a

couple of alien books. "They're from everywhere—different countries, time periods, and maybe worlds. Me and Gideon think they have been doing this for a while."

"I feel the same way," chimed in Simon. "When they were holding me, I was drugged, but I heard conversations from time to time. I think they're trying to find a way to preserve their race. I'm not sure why, but what we see in this city really is what's left of their people. I was in and out, but I'm pretty sure I'm right on this." Simon slumped down in the chair.

I took the books from him and set them on one of the shelves. "Rest a minute, and then we're going for Micah. Maybe Smith was telling the truth, and he'll locate her. But I think we can all agree we shouldn't wait around because he's also a piece of shit."

"Let's go." Simon pushed himself to stand. "We're just wasting time here."

Gideon nodded, and I clenched my fists. The blood was boiling in my veins. I wanted my BFF back, and now that we had Simon, fear had turned into frustration and now to anger. I wanted off this fucking planet, with all my friends with me.

Using our now well-developed ninja approach, we searched the floor for a hidden staircase or elevator. Each room had a master bedroom representing different time periods on Earth, dating back to around the 15th century.

The last room was empty. No stairs, elevator, or other means to get to whatever was above us. Gideon estimated at least four more stories should be accessible judging by the exterior of the semi-skyscraper.

"How did we get back to the desert?" I asked the guys.

"What?" Simon paced the room.

"When we were in the desert house. How did we get from inside back to the desert?"

"We walked through the wall." Gideon turned his head from side to side.

"That's right. How about we give it a try." I rapped on the wall with my knuckles.

Gideon placed his fingertips on the wall opposite me. He trailed them across it as if he were following a map, and Simon tapped with his fist. I was seriously disappointed when none of us found anything, but at least we were doing something.

I sighed, "We have to re-check every room. Any one of them could have a passageway."

The three of us got about halfway through the floor when we found a kitchen that resembled the one from *The Brady Bunch*. The appliances reflected the avocado green finish and matching cabinets that were so popular then. Chrome chairs with burnt orange vinyl seating complimented the glossy white tabletop, and the burnt orange laminate countertops brought it all together. Yep. Marsha and Jan should be moseying on in any minute now.

I propped my elbows up on the brilliant orange counter and rested my chin on my hands. What should have been rigid felt spongy like pound cake. I lifted my arms off the Formica and lightly pressed the palm of my hand down; it sunk slightly into the surface.

"Jess, what are you doing?"

"Feel this countertop; it's weird."

Gideon ran his hands across the surface. "It's kind of squishy."

Simon took a step back from the wall he'd been checking. "You know, nothing is what it seems with these people. If these rooms are just placed here, could it be that what we're looking for is right in front of us, and we just can't see it?"

"Meaning what?" asked Gideon.

I poked the counter with my index finger. "I think if they can transport people, rooms, even whole neighborhoods through time, then they're pretty clever. Do you remember how Micah kept fading in and out? Well, maybe these things are here, but not really. Sort of like a memory of what was. The actual room is still here, and this is just sort of an overlap."

Gideon's bum squeaked across the vinyl seating. "But, if that's true, how can we touch these things? I mean, we can move them around and feel them in our hands. Sit on them. If this is all a memory of the actual items, wouldn't they just fade away if we reached for them?"

"I said I had a theory. I didn't say it was perfect."

"No. It's actually a good thought." Simon tapped his hands together in a soft clap. "We keep thinking in our terms, things we know to be true. But this is a whole different civilization. We assume that they transport things, places, and plop them down where there is nothing. But what if they can also layer? Like a house of cards. One thing on top of the next until you build your house. Or, in this case, room. That would explain your questions about the basement, right, Gideon? You said it looked like something out of the Middle Ages."

"Yeah. I guess it would."

"They obviously have far surpassed what we know about science in our world. Maybe there's a way they can actually do that. It's brilliant, actually, if you think about it," Simon said rapidly. "You could virtually hide anything. Not that I'm saying that was their plan—maybe it was just a bonus to their technology, but it's brilliant, nonetheless. Let's try a different approach. We see these things and our eyes tell us they're solid. We can touch them, move them, even sit on them. But what if it's really just part of the illusion? We believe it, so it is. Close your eyes, clear your mind, and think of a blank space. Now open them. What do you see?"

"Uh—I see the same room we were looking at two seconds ago," I said dryly.

"Try again. Try not to expect to see what you think is there. Look at what's *really* there. Okay, close your eyes again.

Don't think of where you are. If a blank space doesn't work, then think of someplace you love. Picture that place and expect that place when you open your eyes."

"Okay."

"Let's all try."

"Opening my eyes now—crap. What the hell? Do you—" I thought the grounds and the exterior were pretty bland, but now this room bore a striking resemblance to a Barbie house. A large clear plastic-like table in the center of the room with six bulky, king-sized black chairs screamed the 1970s. In the center of the table was a game of some kind that consisted of a round grey board with twelve black sticks about ten inches tall surrounding the outer edge of the circle. In the center of the board were two additional levels, square not round like the first. Monitors displaying pictures of vintage American television shows in black and white from the sixties and seventies covered the wall to the left of us. I'm not sure how The Brady Bunch or the coverage of Watergate fit with their plan, but that's what we were watching. To the right, a lone chair rested in a reclined position and above it, another screen. The art on the three other walls were portraits of people I can only assume were important on their planet. The paintings were like every other décor we'd come across in this strange world, simple black and white with grey accents. Each face was equally void of emotion as the next.

"I see it too." Gideon grabbed my hand. "Just like Simon said. This is a whole different room. Actually, this is more like what I imagined it *would* look like inside."

"Well, this is a new approach. Let's move on."

But despite our optimism, room after room remained unchanged. My shoulders slumped, heavy with disappointment—until we opened one final door. A large staircase rose in the center of what was not a room at all but another hallway with windows. We cautiously approached, and I peered out. The suns were in full bloom, and the alien land sizzled with ripples of heatwaves.

I took the lead as we continued through the house, trying to locate Micah; I'd rather be the head of the snake than the tail. An observation that some might think too dangerous but my desire to get out of this fucking place far exceeded any real fear.

Unlike the previous stairwell, this one was uncomfortably narrow, and my rapid breathing triggered an acid eruption in the pit of my stomach—I hated tight spaces. I closed my eyes and imagined all of us in the car going to California for a weekend of total relaxation on the beach. I could hear the waves crashing into the shore and feel the warmth of the sun on my face. My pulse slowed, and I could take in a full breath, drawing a blanket of calm over my anxious body. I opened my eyes. We were standing at a landing under the peak of the house. There was a solid wall in front of us.

"Okay, now what?" asked Gideon.

Brushing my hand across the wall, I grinned. "Another illusion. Whatever's up here, they've taken great measures to keep it hidden. Feel the wall."

I grabbed his hand and held it against the wall. It gently flexed. "This is what the countertops felt like."

He nodded in agreement. "Only this is much more flexible. Similar to the wall in the attic."

I closed my eyes and opened them. The wall was still there.

"Okay, if it's not really there, how come all I see is this wall?"

"I don't know. Learning as we go here, Jess. Maybe this frequency is stronger than the others. Maybe it's because they wanted to protect this area with everything they have. The only way we are going to find out the answers is to keep going," said Simon.

"What if we attempt to go through and our minds freak?

Seeing the solid wall while we pass through, our minds might believe we're trapped. If we believe it, it's real to us. So, if we believe we're trapped, we're trapped—we die." I raised a brow.

"Don't freak, mate," Simon instructed.

"Oh, simple." I rolled my eyes.

"Close your eyes. You can hold onto my belt loop. I know you hate tight places. If this is like the first wall we passed through, it's like a narrow tunnel."

Claustrophobia is a valid emotion, but I hated feeling dependent. I also knew I could have a panic attack if things felt too tight, and it would slow us down.

"Thanks." I wrapped two fingers around one of Gideon's belt loops and closed my eyes.

I decided to indulge the mall fantasy. There I am, with Micah in the Galleria, close to Henderson and where I live. We're walking, and it's not crowded. We can stop at every window display if we feel like it, but it's around the holidays, and wouldn't it be great to get a hot chocolate and watch the kids with Santa? The Galleria always had the best Santa every year.

I hear the corny songs and smell the pine potpourri in the kiosk next to us. And I know I need a dress. New Year's is just a few weeks away. Micah knows I love black velvet, and she's dragging me to our favorite store, Forever 21.

There's the dress in the window. It's short with a deep V-neck and plenty of bling on the hemline. I press my fingers to the glass—but wait, I forgot to get my mother a Christmas card. We always pick the most special cards for each other, and the mall has this little stationery store—*hey, why did we stop?*

"Listen to me," Gideon was whispering. "We need to stop for a second, but don't open your eyes. Everything's okay. We just need to wait here for a minute."

I'm not sure what made me do it. I don't know if it was stupidity, temptation, or what. But I did exactly the opposite of what Gideon said—I opened my eyes. I immediately heard a horrible, piercing scream.

It was me. I was looking at *everything*—the past and the present were swirling in front of us, behind us, all around, completely consuming my last ounce of sanity. I tried to focus but started to feel dizzy and nauseous. I swayed back and forth. I watched President Lincoln get shot, Martin Luther King march for freedom, what looked like the Revolutionary War. Then, terrifyingly, I saw something that had clearly not happened in our world but looked every bit as tragic as anything from our violent history. It reminded me of pictures of World War II, with hundreds of dead bodies piled on top of each other. Whatever had happened, it was dreadful.

Ghostly silhouettes of men circled around the horror in protective jumpsuits. They looked human, but the landscape clearly told me they weren't. The sky held multiple suns. It was *their* world. Then it started to fade, and all I could see was a wall forming in front of me, becoming more solid by the second. My breathing grew shallow. Darkness filled my head, and I felt myself slipping away.

My entire body shook, no—it was Gideon shaking me. "Jess! Shut your frigging eyes and breathe!

I squeezed my eyes shut. My finger grew numb as I tightened my grip, but I didn't care. "

"What the fuck?" I threw up a little in my mouth.

"Don't know." Gideon's words thundered.

"This is different than before," Simon shouted. "Wait, we're here."

"Jess, we're through; open your eyes." Gideon peeled my fingers from his belt loop.

My lids fluttered to adjust to the fluorescent, overhead lighting. There was no neighborhoods or desert, just a large room the size of a high-school gymnasium. This house was definitely consistent with its inconsistencies.

Like cubicles in an office, small glass-walled booths lined the room, each covered in knobs, buttons, and gadgets. On the floor in the center of room was a large grey circle. In the far-right corner was a door, looking odd among all the glass. We lined up like the Beatles crossing Abbey Road. Gideon reached for the doorknob and hesitated a moment before turning it. *Locked.* Before he had a chance to make a move, I pulled out my utility knife from my back pocket and handed it to him—gift from dad that just keeps on giving.

Waiting for him to pick the lock was a torturous few minutes. My heart pounded against my rib cage. Then, *click.*

Gideon opened the door, and Micah was lying on the bed. I pushed past him and rushed to her side. Pushing back the weighted comforter, I called out to her. Her eyes twitched, and her hand fell over the side of the bed. I sat next to her and tried to scoop my hand under her back to lift her, but her body was limp.

"I think they sedated her like they did you." I turned to Simon.

"We need to get her up and moving. Whatever that junk is they gave us, it's potent. She needs to work it out of her system." Simon took a firm grip on Micah's arm and lifted her. "Here, grab her other arm and help me get her to her feet." Me and Gideon grabbed her arm with one hand, and Gideon lifted from behind her back. When we had her on her feet, we paced around the room.

After a few minutes, she was able to recognize us enough to see the relief on our faces.

I gobbled her up in a tight hug and kissed her cheek.

"You are never gonna believe the things I saw," she said. "I'm telling you crazy, unimaginable shit. There were people, but not from here. I mean not from our time. It was the damn past.

"We know. We've seen it, too," Simon told her.

"You know? What have you seen? Are you sure? Because I'm telling you, I've seen some really trippy stuff."

"You'd be surprised." I curled the corners of my mouth and widened my eyes. "Ever since you left us, we've been searching everywhere in this house. This place is like a funhouse at the carnival. The past is happening all around us. We just can't see it without their time-traveling contraption. What we don't know is how you wound up here."

"Yeah. How did you get here?" Gideon asked. "Did they bring you here, or is this where you wandered to?"

"They brought me here after retrieving me from whatever year I was stuck in. They injected me with something, and the next thing I remember is seeing all of you. That weird-as-hell Mr. Smith is creepy." We all nodded. Smith looked human, but his mannerisms made me feel like he could reach in and suck out my brain.

"Okay, I think we need to go. Are you okay to walk?" I asked.

"I'm okay and so ready to get out of here. I don't mean to cause a ripple in our so far wonderful day, but does anyone know exactly how we plan on finding our way home?"

I rounded my eyes. "I think we go back to the place we came through."

"That's great. But do you remember how to get there? Does anyone?" Micah bit her lower lip.

"I've been keeping a sort of map in my head. I'm pretty sure I remember how to get us back, or at the very least, in the vicinity."

Simon spoke up. "We can't go back yet."

I'm pretty sure my jaw unhinged and dropped to the floor right beside Micah's.

"I know you're all anxious to get the hell out of here. So am I," Simon said quickly. "But what do we tell the authorities when we get back? We still have no idea what they're doing or why. We wouldn't be able to tell them anything of real value. 'Yes, Mr. FBI Man, we met aliens who led us to a doorway to their planet just after they killed my wife and made a whole town appear and disappear in the desert. No, we don't know why they did this or where they come from. No, we have no clue as to their plans or what they want from our planet. Oh, but wait! We can tell you they have this really awesome device that can travel through time and bring objects and people back and forth. Go get them.'"

I hadn't heard Simon sound so sarcastic. He sounded more like...me. We'd ruined him.

"Do you see what I mean?" he continued. "We'll sound ridiculous. We need some sort of answers to take back with us...to prove this very unbelievable story. Am I making sense to all of you? I know everyone's first instinct is to cut and run because, quite frankly, it's mine. But if we don't get some answers, this will have all been for nothing. Catherine's death would be meaningless." We knew with those last five words, we couldn't leave. Damn.

"All right," Gideon relented. "We'll see what we can find out before we get out of here. But if we don't learn anything new soon, we'll have to go without it. My gut tells me that we've been really lucky up until now. Smith could have made things a lot more difficult for us, and he hasn't. I'm not sure why we've been able to elude them the past few hours, but I have a feeling that if we really were a threat to them, we wouldn't be standing here discussing this."

Gideon had a good point.

I nodded. "It's all been kind of easy for us. The way we got away, how we found Simon and Micah. Maybe it's because we really haven't tried to find out what they're up to. I don't know. But once we commit to doing this, I think we'll definitely put ourselves on the no-fly list. We'll need to be stealthy and see what we can find, then get out fast."

We agreed to go back to the large room with the cubicles, but my inner voice gnawed at me, flinging question after question until I had to blurt out my thoughts.

"Wait. No." I stopped. "This is too obvious. Think about it," I said. "We get led all around this house thinking there must be something upstairs—something they are protecting. So, we change our focus and find our way here, where Micah is very conveniently waiting. Remember, all of this is what they want it to be. Rooms from the sixteen-hundreds, kitchens from the nineteen-fifties. Whatever they want to project, they can. So why put Micah in the one place they don't want us to go? The one place that appears to be a control room of some sort." I folded my arms across my chest. "Wouldn't you think they would want to keep her as far away from that room as possible? Maybe in the basement, or better yet, where we started from? After all, we already know what's there. Or do we? What if *that* is the very place they are trying to protect?"

"That makes sense." Micah chimed in. "We never really checked out the house we came through to get here. We were so focused on following them. What if we were in the center of it all right from the start? This house could just be a cover—a storage unit, maybe. The real truth is not in their town, but where it all started for us."

Chills trickled along my spine, and I shivered.

So, back down we went, the clang of our feet on the metal staircase feeling a little like a *come get us* signal to Smith. We moved fairly quickly. I was right. I *did* remember how to get out of that awful house.

It had taken hours of wandering through alien territory before we found our friends, but once I knew the layout, getting out was much quicker. Yay, me and my love of puzzles. Who knew it'd be lifesaving someday?

Once we were out and on the grounds, however, it was a different story. Grey goons surrounded the front of the property like a barrier of testosterone. Wait ... do they have testosterone?

Micah's eyes grew wide as she mouthed, *now what?*

I quickly scanned for cover, ducking behind some tall hedges that lined the side of the property. I fanned my hand for everyone to follow me, and we crouched down, blending in between the charcoal leaves.

As we reached the end of the hedges, we faced a massive, sturdy gate. It was the last barrier to freedom, but before I could move, someone grabbed my shoulder. At first, I thought it was Micah, so I didn't turn. But when the grip became tighter, I knew something was wrong. My heart raced. I knew I had to look but couldn't bring myself to turn.

I called for Gideon in a soft whisper, even though whoever was behind me could clearly hear. Gideon turned, and his wide eyes and gaping mouth made it clear that we were screwed. *Crap!*

Gideon's hand shot out, grabbed my shirt, and yanked me into his chest. We fell to the ground, and as I angled my body, I saw Smith and several grey goons right behind us. Both of us scrambled to our feet. "Run!" I shouted. Micah panted alongside me, the two of us sprinting across the onyx lawn.

"Go for the gate," Simon called.

We darted for the iron gate as the grey goons swarmed to us like a school of fish to breadcrumbs—we were the crumbs. Smith floated across the property, and for a moment, my heart stopped beating. Grey goons blocked the main gate, so we veered left, aiming for the smaller entrance. *Let it be unlocked,* I begged. Fortunately, Smith was too busy calling out commands to his lead-footed troops. The goons thumped their way in our direction like lumbering giants in a child's fairytale.

The gate was still several yards away when I looked over my shoulder. I should have just kept my attention fixed on the gate. A sharp pain drilled into my temples as Smith turned his attention back to us, kicking his glide into high gear.

Simon grabbed Micah. "We need to split up."

"No!" I screamed. But Gideon seized my hand. "Only until we all reach the gate. Keep moving."

Somehow, it worked. A new league of grey goons had forged a wall of flesh in front of us. Me and Gideon darted to the right while Micah and Simon veered left. We zigzagged through the sea of alien hitmen, and for an intellectually superior race, it was obvious none of them were familiar with football. Honestly, it would have been comical if we hadn't been so terrified. We darted, and they, well, they didn't. I followed Gideon as he weaved around them as if they were statues. The looks of perplexity on their faces were comforting.

Finally, we were ahead of them. Smith barked, "Catch them!"

As slow as they were with their legs, their minds calculated a quick solution. Instead of chasing us, they had somehow called for reinforcements. In moments, a new obstacle of aliens hid the gate. Right in front floated our number-one problem—Smith. We were completely blocked off. A full troop of grey goons formed behind us. We exchanged glances of desperation. We were trapped, and Smith knew it. A sneer replaced the anger in his eyes. They had out-thought us again. This was getting old.

We clustered together in the center of the yard between two walls of aliens, standing back to back like the Avengers in the latest Marvel flick. Where's Captain America when you need him? I swallowed against the burning in my throat.

Scanning the mass of goons boxing us in, we saw one maneuver offered a viable solution. We needed to charge them and hope we could fight our way to freedom. Since they're slow, we could use that to our advantage. My real worry was Smith.

"We need to do something, or else we're never getting out of here," I murmured.

Micah butted up to my shoulder, "You still have the utility knife?"

"Yup."

"Use it."

I pulled the steel blade from my pocket and clicked it open. It wasn't much, but it would slice flesh.

"I'll take it," said Gideon.

"My blade, my hands." I glared.

I took point, and we lined up like a set of bowling pins. "Now!" I shouted. The guys flanked me while Micah stayed on my heels. The grey goons trudged down the center and fanned out, focusing on the guys. I wielded my blade, slicing through the air until it landed on the unlucky alien who reached me first.

"Fuck you, you bastard." I sliced across his chest and his cheek.

Micah barreled into him, pushing the injured goon to the ground. Like ants, they came from everywhere, and I searched the mass of hulks covering the lawn and cringed with fear when I saw the true picture unfold. The larger grey goons had their hands on the guys. Gideon punched aimlessly at whatever he could hit while Simon clawed to break free.

One of the goons grabbed me and nearly broke my arm as he bent it behind my back, peeling the blade from my fingers. Micah kicked him, but one of his buddies grabbed her and threw her to the ground. The guys were in the clutches of several goons, struggling to break free. They were fighting a losing battle.

"Take the men in the house," ordered Smith.

The goons led Micah and me to the same large black vehicle that had carried Simon into this hellish trap. We pushed and kicked, but it was futile. The goons definitely learned from their mistakes. These assholes weren't easing up their grip anytime soon.

Reeling against the arms restraining him, Gideon called out, "I'll find you, Jess. They're frigging dead."

My eyes pooled with tears as I continued to struggle against the vice grip on my arm. As they shoved me into the car behind Micah, I chanced one last glance over my shoulder. The windows were tinted, a hollow ache settled in the pit of my stomach as I wondered if I would ever see the guys again.

Micah hooked her arm through mine, pulling me tight against her. The beam from the dome light illuminated her tear-stained cheeks. Where the hell were they taking us?

CHAPTER 12

PROMISES

THE WARM METALLIC taste on my lips overshadowed the throbbing in my arm. I wiped my mouth with the back of my hand, the crimson smear staining my flesh.

Micah's face burned red, her anger directed to the hulks in the front seat. "You're a despicable race of people."

Ever since they shoved us into the car, they hadn't said one word to either of us. In fact, they hadn't said anything at all. They just sat there, stone-faced and silent—the perfect pair of robotic idiots.

"You know you two are so much fun, but I think me and my friend have had enough jokes for today," I mocked them. "No, no, stop, please. You're hilarious."

Nothing. Not even a look in the rear-view mirror.

"I don't think they get your humor." Micah leaned her head against the window.

"You think?

"I'm thinking they're either deaf or stupid. Could be both." We were joking, but I knew by her widening eyes, Micah's anger was swiftly turning to fear. My left hand throbbed, then subsided to a numbing tingle under her grip.

"You didn't answer, my friend," I taunted. "Where are you

taking us? Oh, come on. It's not like it'll be a secret once we get there. We can't go anywhere. Why can't you just tell us?"

The grey goon in the passenger seat turned and glared at the two of us. Finally— acknowledgment.

"Are you going to tell us?" I pressed further.

He sucked in a deep breath. He sounded exasperated. It was nice to know the two of us were getting to him. "You're both going back to the desert neighborhood."

The driver whipped his head sharply to the right. "Don't say anything. He told us to keep quiet and just drive them back."

Scared or not, they were starting to really get on my nerves. And when I get agitated, I get mouthy.

"Who? Smith? What, is he your boss? Does he tell you everything to do? Do you listen to everything he says? Wow. He must be, like, really special or something. Micah, I think Smith must be their leader."

"I think you might be right. It was pretty obvious back at the house that everyone listened to him, and only him." We continued to banter until the goon in the passenger seat, clearly on edge, reached back and swung for me. Good thing I was far enough back that he missed, but the driver got angry and pulled over.

"Get out of the car." He pointed to his passenger's door. The man didn't even argue. He just got out and stood by the side of the road. As the door shut, Micah and I grinned at each other, victorious.

Then there was one.

The closer we got to the entry house, the more the surroundings became familiar. A sparse patch of desert circled the block of houses. Seeing that setting made everything feel all too real; I ached to get back home. Micah slowly blinked like she was trying to erase the view, and I bumped her shoulder and mouthed out, *love you*. We rounded a corner and parked in front of the house where our journey had begun.

"Get out and go inside." The massive grey goon didn't even bat an eye. He was so stiff, if a good wind came along, he'd just break in two. We lingered in front of the house, and Micah leaned in and whispered in my ear.

"We are not going in there to cheerfully be murdered. We should run for it. Anything is better than just doing what they tell us."

I nodded. The last thing I wanted to do was nothing. We needed to act, or we would never get home.

"I don't have a plan other than running. If you got something better, let me know," Micah whispered.

"I got nothing. Let's go." Micah nodded, and we made a break for it. I followed Micah down the block. I had expected her to go for the desert, but instead, she veered left and darted through the side yard of one of the bigger houses.

The grey goon ran after us, but he was slow. In a few seconds, he was trailing far behind us.

A five-foot-high cinder block fence surrounded us. It wasn't easy, but we managed to scrape and yank ourselves over the top. Our newly found skill to scale concrete helped us conquer several more as we scrambled to the next yard and then the next, trying to lose our alien hunter.

After sprinting through five yards, we tried the sliding glass door on one of the houses. Discovering it locked, Micah scrambled around the right side of the house, and I went left. I found a small window that could be a bathroom. I slid it along the track—bingo. I ran to grab Micah, and we scampered through the window, finding ourselves sharing a bathtub with the shower curtain drawn back. The door stood wide open. Across the hallway was a bedroom. I had that feeling, again, that if I didn't know any better, this could be just another house back home. After several minutes of checking in closets and under beds, we knew we were alone.

"I don't know why they separated us, but I got a bad feeling."

I couldn't resist. "Oh, you think?"

She shot me a glare.

"Sorry."

"Me too." Micah slid down the wall and landed on the tan, shag carpet. "Whatever they want from us involves this neighborhood. Somehow, we need to find the guys. We can sort things out once we're safe."

"We need to get the keys to the car."

Her eyes narrowed. "You've completely lost your mind. How the hell are we gonna get the keys?"

"I didn't say it would be easy."

"It'll be impossible."

"We'll have to knock him out."

Her mouth gaped, and her eyes bulged. "What? No! That's not a plan."

"If we can get the car, then we can find the guys and get back here faster. On foot, we're easy prey."

Micah huffed, "All right. What'd got in mind?"

We searched the house for something heavy enough to knock the grey goon unconscious. We found a well-worn small but sturdy shovel in the garage.

I picked it up and swung it a few times to test the weight. Then Micah tried. We both agreed it felt heavy enough to do the job but manageable enough for us to swing.

"I'm gonna knock him out." Micah gripped the handle.

"Okay, I'll lure him to you."

We headed down the street, me in plain view while Micah followed just a few feet out of sight, creeping along the front lawns of the homes. Thank goodness for the thick cover provided by the trees and bushes.

I got about halfway down the block before he spotted me and came running—his version of running anyway. For a race that could time travel, they really needed to work on their reflex speed.

I didn't want to appear completely obvious, so I tried to dart back and forth as if I was trying to avoid him. When he was close enough to reach out for me, I let him grab me. Micah burst from the bushes, ran behind him, and slammed him in the head with the shovel. His grip loosened, and I broke free.

Stunned, he fell to his knees—and then got right back up. Micah just stood there, shocked. As the goon grabbed the shovel out of her hands, I grabbed Micah by the shirt, and we ran.

"The trash can." I pointed.

We both made a dash for it. I grabbed it first and ran screaming at the goon to keep him occupied. Micah circled behind him and pushed as hard as she could. For a moment, he was off balance.

Bam! I heaved the aluminum can into his head. He fell to his knees, and this time I didn't wait.

Bam! Bam! Bam!

I hit him until he fell face down in the middle of the road. Micah quickly rummaged through his pockets and found the keys. Not bothering to look back, we beat it out of there and didn't stop until safely encased in the alien vehicle. *Did I say safe?* The damn thing had no instruction, pictures, or visible ignition. At least the steering wheel was there. I studied the dash for a moment; it was a long screen that ran the width of the car. I touched it, and lights came on. There were icons in the shape of what resembled some of the necessities. I poked the one that looked like an ignition, and the screen flipped up and revealed a working dashboard. I fit the key in and started it up. Searching for the accelerator, I was thrilled to see two familiar pedals under the dash. I took a shot and gingerly pressed my foot down on the right side. The engine revved. Yes!

We made it back to the house in record time, parking a few blocks away. Neither of us had any idea how long the alien giant would be unconscious, but eventually, he would wake. The chromatic foliage adorning the front of each home reminded me of a black rose I'd seen once in a photography magazine. The delicate flower cast a shade of blue, a color accent wasted on the residents of this planet. Its stark beauty struck me. If this experience wasn't so traumatizing, I might have really enjoyed the stroll. *Jeez, Jessie, snap back.* I recalled the events of the past few days, and the view quickly lost its appeal.

Approaching the tall building, we saw at least a dozen hulk-like goons spread out across the lawn. "Let's try for the little gate," I whispered to Micah.

We snuck around to the side of the property. Like earlier, the goons left this treasure unguarded. Hoisting myself up, I scraped my sneakers along the concrete wall and over the fence. My stomach gurgled its way to a nauseous anger.

When we got to the door of the house, I held my breath. *Whew—unlocked.*

I pushed the door slightly ajar and peeked in. The room appeared empty. We slipped in and shut the door. A sage-like aroma tickled my nose, a scent I didn't notice the last time we were here. We navigated through the chef-sized kitchen by a narrow beam of daylight cast through a small rectangular window.

My T-shirt snagged on the corner of a prep table. As I freed myself, my hand brushed the cold stainless steel.

"You need help?" Micah asked.

"No, I got it." I pulled my shirt free, tearing the hemline in the process.

We found the hallway and hesitantly opened the first door. It took a second for our eyes to adjust in the dimly lit room. Gideon and Simon were sitting in chairs, bound, and gagged.

Instinct kicked in, and without assessing our surroundings, we ran to free them. We should've approached more cautiously. Micah pulled Simon's tape off first, and as she did, he shouted, "No, get out! It's a trap! Smith is waiting..."

We turned as Smith glided through the door, followed by six of the grey goons. *Damn.* We scrambled to maneuver around them, but it was impossible. We were back in his clutches.

"I told you before that we cannot let you leave," said Smith angrily. "You women are possibly the key to the continued existence of our race. Your species is the closest to our own. It is basic survival."

"Basic survival? What the hell are you talking about?

Smith glided back a few feet, clasping his hands. I could tell he was uncomfortable.

"Our world is dying. Many years ago, creatures came to our planet. They were peaceful, but they carried a deadly virus to our people. The females that survived became infertile." Smith's chin dropped. "Human DNA is the only one similar to our own."

"What are you saying?" I clenched my fists.

"We have been trying to blend our species. The neighborhoods you saw were for the incubation period. An attempt to keep the host calm. Their memories are temporarily erased while they carry the child."

I struggled to process what he'd just said, it felt like a nightmare, and I kept waiting to wake up.

"Wait ... so you're making human and alien babies?"

"We have not been completely successful."

"You're a race of monsters! What happens to the women?"

"Most of them are returned to their family, their memories restored to a time before the experiment."

"And the ones that don't?" I inched closer; I wanted to punch him in the face.

Smith cleared his throat, stiffened his posture, and spoke in a flat tone. "I do what I have to."

"Like Simon's wife? Is that what killed her? Your experiments?"

Smith was no longer answering questions. He addressed the grey goons. "Take them all back to the desert, and we will begin immediately." He turned back to Micah and me; his cold stare gave me chills. "Both of you have made this far more difficult than need be. If you two cooperate, we will send your friends back."

Micah and I exchanged glances. Being an incubator to these alien creeps was not on my to-do list but saving Gideon and Simon was. Maybe this would buy us time to figure out an exit plan, or maybe it just meant the guys would get back home. Either way, they'd be safe.

"You promise to let the guys leave, and you won't get any more trouble from either one of us. We'll cooperate." Gideon and Simon struggled to break their restraints. "Gideon. Simon. Stop. There is no other choice."

"Bloody hell, there isn't!"

"Simon's right. You can't just give in. Don't do it." For the first time, I saw genuine fear on Gideon's face.

Micah shook her head and glared at Smith. "You promise?" He nodded. I joined her, and she grabbed my hand. "Okay then, we're ready."

"Wait," I said. "Cut them loose."

Smith nodded to one of the alien goons. The hulkish soldier took a large blade from his belt and cut the binding from the guys. Gideon immediately took a charging stance, and I stepped in front of him.

"This is the only way."

"Like hell it is."

I reached down and clasped his hand. Sapphire met chestnut as I gazed into his eyes. I need a goodbye.

"You need to go, finish what we wanted to do. I'll be okay if I know you're safe."

"Jessie, I can't ..."

"You can."

I stood on my toes, my lips drinking in one last kiss.

"Enough. Get them out of here." Smith ordered.

The goons led us to a charcoal grey sedan, and I could hear the guys screaming our names and a few other choice words while even more of Smith's men shoved them unwillingly into a black SUV. A transparent plastic panel separated us from the front of the car. The windows had a dark tint, making the outside world look even blacker. I felt numb. The butterflies and jitters that had been tormenting my stomach had stopped. Everything became quiet. I looked over at Micah. Her head leaned on the glass, and she gazed out the window. I saw no hint of emotion in her face, and I figured she must be feeling just as numb as me. I didn't know what our fate would be, but at least the guys were safe and would be going home. Maybe they could get someone to believe our story and come back to help us. Maybe not.

Smith sat in the front seat with a grey goon driver. They whispered a few words here and there, but nothing I could actually understand. I wasn't worried that he would do anything to harm us. It was pretty clear by now that he needed us. So, I decided to push the envelope—again.

"You owe us the truth." He turned and glared at me but didn't say a word. "I said, *glider of gloom*, you owe us. You've gotten your way, and we're coming with you willingly. The least you can do is tell us our fate."

"I have told you."

"Have you? You said some return home. What happened to the children they bore?"

"What does it matter to you?"

"You're taking our people. It means everything to me."

Smith gripped the dash. His agitation was my pleasure.

"Very well. Our fetuses gestate very quickly compared to yours. In seven days, they are mature enough to be taken from the host. The female and her family are then returned to their normal lives. We usually take over a block or even a neighborhood at a time. So, you see, to them, everything appears quite normal. They do not have any memory of the pregnancy."

"Okay, so you get them pregnant, and they give you a child. You said your entire planet was dying out. That can't be enough to get the whole race rebooted. What are you not telling us?"

Smith cleared his throat and put his hands to his mouth for a moment, sort of like he was praying. I knew that wasn't happening, but still, it looked— human. "We then take those children and duplicate them tenfold."

That was enough to get Micah's attention and knock her out of her silent stupor.

"You clone them!" she cried. "You take those babies, and you clone them? Is there no end to how sick in the head you people are? What do you tell them?" Micah tapped her foot so hard, I thought she'd put a hole in the floorboard.

Smith looked perplexed. "Who?"

"The children, you idiot. What do you tell them when they see nine other people running around looking exactly the same as they do?"

"We don't. We spread them out to various towns, and they know nothing of the beginnings of their existence. The few deaths we've had to endure were minuscule compared to saving the entire planet. I know it is unacceptable to you, but this was our only choice."

"No. No, it wasn't. You could've chosen to keep looking to your own resources for a cure. But you didn't. You said our people were young when you first started coming. How long has this been happening to us? How long have you been raping the women on our planet?" I kicked the back of his seat.

"We do not rape your females. That would imply violence. We are not a violent people. Rather the opposite. We have gone to great measures to make this process the least disruptive possible."

"How long?"

"Ten centuries, by your time."

It took me a minute to calculate. But Micah whipped her head around like that girl from *The Exorcist*.

"*A thousand years*?" she cried. "How? Why? Don't you freaks have your population back yet?"

I wanted to break the divide and wrap my fingers around the pompous bastard's neck. His casual demeanor about the demise of innocent humans created pictures in my mind I didn't even know I was capable of doing. I squeezed my eyes shut, wincing tighter to push away the murderous thoughts that came at me one by one—all ways to slaughter Smith.

"We have grown to a considerable number, yes. But whatever has infected us infects the new children too. We had hoped your DNA would resolve the issue, but it has not. So twice a year, we perform this ritual. This ensures the perpetuation of life on our planet while we continue the search. You see, we haven't given up. We have just been forced to take other measures."

"And did your people ever think that the reason you haven't found the solution is because there isn't one? You're clearly an advanced race; you've crossed worlds. Surely it occurred to you that there are no more options. You've been searching a thousand years. When will you stop?"

"We will never stop trying. We cannot."

"No matter what the cost? Who *are* your people now anyway? They're not you, they're not us, so who are they? What you all fail to realize is that the race you've been fighting so hard to preserve has been gone for a very long time."

"Enough. You asked me to tell you what your purpose was, and I have. There will be no more conversation. We will be there soon, and your process will begin. In two weeks' time, you will be back home and have no memory of this."

"Wait. You're sending us home?"

"Yes."

"But I thought you said you couldn't let us go. Why the change of heart?"

"There has been no change of heart. We fully intended to return you to your home. I merely said that in hopes of crushing your spirit so you'd stop fighting us. Instead, it had the opposite effect—you fought harder. You are such a strange emotional species. I told you we are not a violent people. We are merely surviving."

"Yeah. You're a regular humanitarian."

"Enough. We are almost there."

"I have one more question." I figured why not go for broke. "Something's been bugging me."

"What?" Smith's temple pulsated.

"How come everything in your city is in Earth English? I mean all the store fronts and prices in the windows...it's all like home."

"It is to you."

"What the fuck does that mean?" Micah chimed in.

"It means, our technology adjusts to the aliens and their speech. It heard your language and translated it to what you saw in the city."

"And still you can't find a cure. Sounds to me like you need to get your priorities straight."

Smith just sat in silence. I'd like to think I made him reflect on what I said, but I doubt it.

A few minutes passed, and I turned to look out the back window. I don't know why, but looking back from where we had come made me feel closer to the guys. Even though Smith said he had intentions of letting us go, the idea that a child I bore would never know their mother and was half ... the tears pooled in the corner of my eyes, I hated Smith and everyone on his planet that thought like him.

My vision blurred, and I dabbed my eyes on the bottom of my T-shirt. I saw a dot in the distance heading in our direction. As it got closer, the shape took form. A large, black SUV was swiftly gaining speed. The closer it got to us, the faster it seemed to go.

I tapped Micah's hand and gestured to the back window. She swiveled and then turned back to me with a smile on her face. Once I had a clear view of the front seat, our situation completely changed. Gideon was driving, with Simon next to him.

The blood raced through my veins, fanning the heat growing in my belly. I glanced at our driver and Smith. They were engaged in conversation, a language I heard for the first time. It vaguely reminded me of Latin with a click of the tongue thrown in between words.

I turned my head and peered over my shoulder. Simon crossed his arms over his chest. Micah poked my waist and tapped her finger on the buckle beside me. She quietly pulled her seat belt out and locked it in place. I did the same. She looked back at Simon and nodded.

The car jolted, and we thrust forward. Smith and the driver didn't turn around.

"Relax," I whispered to Micah. "It will help with the impact."

"You think he's going to do it again?"

"I know he is." We got hit again, and my relaxation techniques went out of the window. Well, at least my seat belt held me securely in place.

"What is going on?" Smith turned to look behind us; his face glowed like the tip of Rudolph's nose. We weren't quite sure exactly what Smith was capable of doing, but something told me we were about to find out.

Bam! Gideon hit us again. *Is he trying to force the driver to pull over?*

Bam! This was starting to hurt.

Our driver made a quick right and then a left, but the guys managed to keep up.

"If you people want violence, I can accommodate." Smith barked.

Our car slowly levitated off the road. I tilted my head back and looked up at the pewter ceiling of the sedan. When I was little, my dad said it was the best way to ease flip flops in your stomach, and mine was attempting a triple twist. Floating into the atmosphere until we were level with the canopy of the surrounding trees, I gripped the door handle until my knuckles were a pasty white. I peered down to the idling SUV, the look of horror on Gideon's face as he gazed up at us most assuredly mirrored the one on mine. We were going to be lost, and the guys would never find us.

In that instant, I made a decision. If I had thought it through, I probably wouldn't have done it. But in the blink of an eye, I undid my seatbelt and reached over to release Micah's belt as well. I opened my door and grabbed her hand. She fixed her wide eyes on me and smirked.

And then we jumped.

I wasn't sure how high we were, but I felt the pressure of

the air slightly contorting my face before the full bough of an onyx pine slowed us down. I hit the ground with my feet and fell backward with a resounding thud, momentarily knocking the wind out of me. I lifted my head in time to see the guys sprinting toward us. Somewhere through the ringing of my ears, I heard Micah ask me if I was okay, but I hadn't fully caught my breath, and the words were left silent on my lips.

When a full breath finally made its way to my lungs, I gasped as the shadow of our abandoned sedan dropped from the sky. The two of us rolled in separate directions, narrowly escaping a painful death. We quickly struggled to our feet as I felt Gideon's powerful arms scoop me up and plunk me down in the backseat of the SUV. Micah nearly bounced off the front seat as Simon threw her in. The stress of nearly suffering a horrible fate took its toll a few miles away. Salty tears stung my cheeks and eyes, and I couldn't control the shakes that had seized my body. Gideon had his arms around me and gently kissed the top of my head.

"You okay?" Gideon asked.

"Y-y-y-yeah. Just need to stop shaking."

He squeezed a little tighter.

"We're going home. We stop for no one, and we don't let anything stop us."

"Sounds good."

"What, no sarcasm about how that's not a plan?"

"No. I'm too tired."

I laid my head on his shoulder and closed my eyes. I knew Smith would be after us, but Gideon was right. This time no bargains. We don't stop until we're home.

CHAPTER 13

THE EXPERIMENTS

I WAS on the other side of the glass of yet another car window, peering at the world around me, and couldn't help but think of the people—not Smith or the large grey goons, but the ordinary, everyday people of this world. The ones who got up each morning, or in this world, every night, and went to work, dropped their kids off at school, shopped at the grocery store, or bought a new outfit for a dinner date. What do they *really* think? How much are they allowed to know about the babies that come into their world? What about Smith—is he a leader?

The questions flooded my head, and the more I asked, the more I realized we really had no answers at all.

Smith told us what he wanted us to know. Beyond that, this planet was as much a mystery to us as when we first got here.

Yellow radiant beams from a distant moon danced along the roofs of the oncoming houses. I wondered what our parents must be thinking. My mom must have called the National Guard by now. If she goes one day without hearing from me, she hits the panic button. But after several days— she's probably on the brink of being committed. I hated the thought of causing her so much pain. Soon we'd be home, I hoped, and everything would be okay. I wasn't sure if I believed what I was thinking or if I was just trying to fool myself.

We pulled into the neighborhood and parked in front of the first row of houses. It made me think of the block where I grew up. My parents have lived there for twenty years, just a short walk from the elementary school. They bought the house when I was about two, so it's the only home I really know. And just like this row of houses, all the ones on my block looked the same.

I remembered growing up and seeing pictures of places like Vermont or Connecticut. Those homes had character and history, and the greenery—so beautiful. Now don't get me wrong, I love the beauty of the desert. The sunsets paint breathtaking skies. But there was something about those unique old structures with their welcoming porches that I loved.

Right now, though, all I wanted was my little cookie-cutter apartment and maybe a cheeseburger. I was starving.

We peeled from the car into the chilly night air. I squinted and turned to Micah. She tightly crossed her arms over her body, and she was shaking. The breath puffed past my chattering teeth as I danced back and forth from one foot to the other.

"It's fucking freezing. How is it just last night it was sweltering, and tonight feels like the Arctic circle? This damn planet is so weird." I tucked my ice-cold nose into my shirt collar and blew warm breath.

"It is the season."

Crap. We all spun around to see Smith hovering no more than ten feet away. *How the hell did he do that?* There were no grey goons in sight.

"Stay the hell away from us." Gideon stepped up beside

Simon and me. "We're done with you, Smith. Whatever extra shit—powers you have, just try and stop us. We are going home—all of us."

"I must say, Gideon, I was surprised to see that you were able to break free from our guards. They are quite large."

"Let's just say they may be big, but they're not very bright."

"That is true. We have never really had any kind of confrontation that warranted combat. Your species, however, has had much experience with the perils of war."

"No one wants war; it's about preparation. Those skills are the reason we're all standing here together instead of becoming yet another victim of your experiments. Your men were clearly outsmarted. Tell us, were they all yours? Or were they the clone creations that you've brought into this world? Either way, you're so screwed, dude."

"Your primitive mindset is one of the reasons we were able to conduct our experiments for such a long time. You say it would be better to know war or something like it. But we have managed to exist in peace throughout our time on this planet. We have grown, intellectually and technologically, far beyond your people. And to answer your question, they are full-blooded Kamarien."

"Kama—what?"

"Kamarien. That is what my people are called. This planet, our planet, is called Kamaria. We are not, what did you say, screwed? The crossbreeds and clones have created a superior race. Those people hold high positions within our government. Mixing your DNA and ours has resulted in a people not only smart but so much more. Don't you see? This melding of our species can benefit both of our worlds."

I interjected. "That very well may be. But don't you think you should have asked us first? Our people should have been given the choice. But you just took what you needed with no regard for us or how it might affect those you used. Are you sure that your people are so peaceful? Because, Smith, it sounds like war to me."

"We're going home. There's nothing you can do to stop us." Gideon tightened his jaw. "Even if we don't all get away, you'll never get the girls—ever." The guys formed a wall in front of Micah and me.

A cry stuck in the back of my throat as Smith swiped his hand, and the guys catapulted into the abyss, swirling in a terrifying free fall before slamming into solid ground. I gasped at the sight of their lifeless bodies.

My heart kick-started when I saw Gideon move his arms underneath his chest and push himself to a sitting position. Simon folded his legs and pulled himself up on his knees. Pushing his feet into the dirt, Gideon wobbled as he stood .

"I told you, Smith, you won't stop all of us." Gideon and Simon stumbled to our side.

Try as I might to focus, my mind started wandering. How come those grey goons, pure Kamarien, couldn't move things? They were much bigger than Smith and, although not completely dumb, much more naïve. Why was he the only one who could do this? How come—

Shit.

I pushed past the guys. "Let me get through. I need to ask him something."

"Jess, no." Micah took my hand.

"It's okay. Just let me get a little closer."

"You're not just a half-breed—you're a creation, a clone. You're that thing we saw back at the house before we got here. When we were in the desert. The freak that chased us. You wanted us to come here. You led us to the gateway. But you look different. This is what *really* happens when you mix the species and clone. How do you hide yourself? How do you do that? How many are there like you?"

"That's not important," he said. "What's important is—"

"How many?" My chest puffed. If there were more like him, how could we really stop them? My muscles trembled but not with fear. It was hate coursing through my body. "Smith, you piece of crap. How many are there like you?"

"Thousands."

Nausea churned my gut and as I swiped my palms on the side of my jeans. *Thousands?* We have to get home. We have to make them listen.

"You won't continue with this," I said. "Now that we know, everyone is gonna hear about you and what you've been doing to us. Our people will stop you."

"Well, that is very unlikely. Now that you have given us so much trouble, we won't be able to let you go. And this time, unfortunately, I do mean it."

My gaze traveled from Micah to Gideon and then Simon. I sliced my index finger across my throat. They returned a brief nod.

We heard a noise and turned. Coming down the road, about five or six minutes away, were several cars. Best guess was that each one was full of grey goons. Whatever we were going to do, it had to be now.

I charged Smith, but his wave was faster than my feet. I skidded across the desert landscape into a thicket of Brittlebush. Micah and Simon came from behind, startling Smith with a barrage of large rocks they'd scooped from the desert. He collapsed to the ground, and Gideon finished the attack with several punches to his head and face.

We ran halfway down the block, and I made a quick left and sprinted for the only two-story house that had its front door wide open.

I abruptly stopped at the stone walkway. Uneasiness roiled my gut. *Why was the door open?* "Something's off. Follow me." I led them around the house to the backyard. We took cover in the shed—one of those prefabricated wood ones you see in front of Lowe's. It was pretty large, a 10 foot by 10 foot and high enough for Gideon to stand upright without being anywhere near the top. To keep our voices at a minimum, I gathered all of us in a huddle.

"The front door is wide open." I tucked my hair behind my ears. "This is the right house, they've just confirmed it, but someone is already here. We need to enter through the back and get to the second story to reach the gateway."

Micah frowned.

"What is it?"

"We never got any proof this place exists. No one is going to believe us," Micah said. She was right. I wouldn't believe this story—why should anyone else?

Simon reached into the deep pocket of his cargo pants and pulled out a small book tattered with age and use. "You think this might help?"

I stretched out my hand, and Simon handed it to me. I opened it and raised a brow. "You're brilliant."

Simon flashed a Cheshire cat grin.

"Simon—dude, that was awesome." Gideon gave him a fist bump.

"Look what I did." Gideon whipped out his phone.

I glared.

"No, don't look at me like that. Here, check it out." Gideon handed me his phone.

He had dozens of photos of the planet, the sky, the plant life, and best of all, from inside the house. We had our proof. All we needed to do now was well, get home.

I handed the phone back to him and faintly smiled. "You did good."

A row of five French doors was at the back of the house, and I hoped at least one of them would be open.

The four of us crept out of the shed to the back patio. We

each tried a handle. It looked grim until Simon pressed down the lever on the last door. With a push and a grunt, it opened, and the rest of us slipped into a partially lit room. In a low whisper, I relayed my thoughts. "Let's try to get upstairs. The top level of this house is the conduit to home. What scares me is we'll be allowed to cross over but not know where we might end up. They obviously control these gateways, and we've caused them plenty of grief. It wouldn't be that difficult for them to send us out into the universe where we can no longer upset their plans and tell anyone what we know."

"I don't think so," said Micah. "I think the houses were built for Las Vegas. Kind of like each room in the big house was designed to reflect the time period that the portal led to."

"Yes. That makes sense." Gideon looked around the room. "This is an average middle-class suburban desert home. We should wind up near Primm since that's where their victims are taken from."

Simon chimed in. "That sounds great, but we won't know for sure until we actually use it. Bollocks, we could end up anywhere."

"There's that, but I think we can try something else," I said. "Remember the room we walked through before the portal, the one we called the directory, with all the images and time periods? Maybe we could have chosen where we wanted to go just by stepping into it at the right moment. It could just be a matter of timing."

"Uh, I'm not so sure I understand or want to understand what you're getting at." Micah knitted a brow. "Are you suggesting we go in blind? Leaping into the one we *think* is our world? Because I've got to tell you, that's a lousy plan."

Simon curled up his mouth and shook his head. "You're partially right. Not us—just me, mate."

"Oh, wait, you are *not* doing this alone. We don't

separate," I insisted. "We go through together. Besides, if you pick the wrong one, how are we going to know?"

"I'll come right back, and then we all go."

I didn't like it, but he'd made a valid point.

"It's our best shot at getting home," Simon sighed. "If anyone has a better plan, then, by all means, let's hear it right now. We're running out of time."

Exasperated, we tiptoed to the stairs, climbing each one with reservation. No one followed us or came busting through the front door—all the more reason to believe that our assumption was correct. They planned on dumping us off in some strange world so we could never tell anyone on our planet what we knew.

Simon held his head high, his shoulders squared. I, on the other hand, was freaked out enough for the both of us. I had wished we had never gone to Primm that weekend or even left Las Vegas. We'd still be floating along through our mundane, happy little existence, none the wiser.

When we found the room, Simon went in first with me on his heels. I peered into every corner. Even the slightest shadow took on the form of an ominous capture. Luckily, my brain was on overdrive because there was no one there.

"Hey, does anyone remember what happened to us the first time we passed through the wall to get here?" No one spoke up. "Really? We looked like a side of beef being sectioned for steaks."

Micah was the first to have the light bulb go off. "Oh, yeah." The guys slowly nodded.

"Well, that didn't happen at the big house."

Micah retorted. "You're right. I don't remember seeing that. Is this something we should worry about?"

Simon interrupted. "We have no time for this. I don't know if it's important or not. But if we don't try this soon, we are undoubtedly never getting home." He reached out for the wall and passed his hand through. Turning to us with smiling eyes, he nodded and then disappeared.

Pacing the room for his return, the door to the room flung open and slammed against the wall. Smith.

I stepped forward. "Man, you're like a bad day that keeps coming back over and over. Give it up; you're gonna lose. We'll get home and tell everyone." I stepped back, growing the distance between me and the gene stew.

"That may be, but you and your friends cannot stop us. When will you realize this is far bigger than any of you imagine?" He floated off the ground, hovering about three feet in the air. Another fucking parlor trick. "We *let* you get away. We *let* you discover some of our secrets. We had hoped that with a better understanding, you would begin to realize our plight and perhaps help willingly."

"Are you trying to pat yourself on the back for going the extra mile?" I asked heatedly. "Do you somehow feel that you've been kind or generous to us by tricking us before you rape our women?" Smith began to squirm again. Apparently, he really took issue with me accusing his species of rape.

Too bad. I wasn't stopping. I stiffened my legs and clenched my fists at my side. "You're not noble, Smith. There is nothing about any of this that is okay. What you and your people have done is dreadful, plain, and simple. You don't get kudos for going the extra mile. You're a vile man. Hell, I don't even know if I can call you a man. What are you? I guess it doesn't matter. We will stop you, and your people will die out, and it won't be because of us. It will be because of your own arrogance."

Smith paused for a moment, and then with an annoyed flick of his hand, sent Micah straight into the wall behind us. Stunned, Gideon and I scrambled to her side. I breathed a sigh of relief when I realized she was only dazed.

"What the fuck's wrong with you? She wasn't mouthing off."

"Yes, but you see, the pain you felt watching your friend get hurt is minuscule to what I feel watching my people perish. Go home, scream alien. They will lock you up."

"You might be right. They might not listen, but..." I was interrupted by Simon's re-entry.

Gideon murmured, "Good?"

Simon nodded.

I was in the *we're gonna get home* happy place, but my relief quickly faded when four grey goons walked in. One of them whispered into Smith's ear. He nodded and glided out of the room, leaving his troops behind.

"Blimey." Simon's voice cracked with frustration.

Gideon followed his eyes and saw the grey goons. I expected him to look as concerned as Simon, but instead, he smirked. "Fantastic."

"Many words came to mind, mate, but fantastic surely wasn't one of them."

Gideon let his arm fall loose to his side and slightly waved his hand for us to move in closer. He whispered, "Diversion."

The goons stood at the doorway like a mountain of bodybuilders, their expression blank.

"Mate, this portal goes straight to the desert house."

"Shit. Finally, something in our favor."

"Okay. Let's go home." We broke up and scrambled in different directions. It took a second to register with the grey goons, and by then, we were rushing the portal. I stopped at the wall and looked back just as Smith came floating back in. Simon picked up a chair, flinging it toward Smith. The bastard swiftly glided to the side as the chair smashed into pieces against the wall.

Gideon circled around the room, running head-on toward Smith with all four grey goons behind him. He darted away at the last second, and with their lack of agility, the hulks smashed into Smith.

Reacting instantly, Smith turned toward Gideon and flicked him headfirst into the wall. My world froze. I wanted to scream for Gideon to please get up, *get up*, but I didn't get a chance. Micah yanked me, and we both went through the portal.

When we arrived at the desert house, I clenched my fists as I dashed to the window. There beyond the landscape was Primm, beckoning us to safety. I sighed a breath of relief.

That is until I realized that Gideon and Simon hadn't come through yet.

I fiddled with my fingers, and Micah paced back and forth, her head down.

"Micah."

She looked up quickly and scanned the room until she caught my stare. I walked over and gave her a hug to reassure her, but truth be told, I wasn't sure myself if they were coming back.

The only thing I could think about was all the time Gideon and I had wasted and the stupid things that had come between us.

As I stood powerless, I quietly prayed for the first time since I was a kid.

Apparently, the universe was listening.

Gideon and Simon came crashing through the wall, rolling onto the floor. In the seconds it took Micah and me to get to them, they were already bouncing back on their feet.

"Run!" Simon yelled, and we all aimed for the stairs. We fled down each step, skimming each other's arms and bodies, flocking in a jumbled descent to freedom.

"Smith is coming, and he has back-up," Simon panted. "They're probably a minute, if not seconds, behind us. We've got to get to the hotel room."

"We need to shut down the portal," I yelled.

"Anyone—know—how?" Micah blurted in between breaths.

"We stop it at the source." My lungs burned. "Room 629."

"She's right," Gideon's size elevens clomped on the sand. "We gotta destroy it."

My head whipped around in his direction. I liked this plan.

Tracking our way across the desert to the hotel, I looked back and saw Smith running, not floating, our way. The grey goons were on his heels.

We crossed the freeway and ran to the front entrance of the casino. We had to go through the gaming area to get to the hotel elevators.

When we got to the lobby, I paused. "Stop." Catching my breath before I continued. "We need to be aware of everyone. Remember, Smith has his people here too. Slow down and act naturally. The more we blend in, the quicker we'll get upstairs unnoticed."

"Wait. We can't go up yet." Simon grabbed Gideon's arm and pulled him back. "We need to figure out what we're going to use to demolish the room. Considering our time crunch, I think a fire is our best bet."

"A fire?" I was all for cutting our connection, but a fire would risk everyone in the hotel and maybe the casino, too. "That's too dangerous. There are innocent people in here."

Gideon took my hands. He looked into my eyes, and I knew—there wasn't any other way. "We can warn them. What if after we start the fire, we clear out the floor? We can't pull the alarm because the sprinklers will go off, but we can bang on their doors as we're running out."

Gideon shook his head. "No ...wait. A fire won't work. If it's just a fire, then the sprinklers will detect the smoke and automatically go off. It could save the room before it does enough damage. What we really need is an explosion. Something that will do so much damage to the room that when the sprinklers go off, it won't matter."

"An explosion? That could kill everyone on the floor." Our plan was going from bad to worse.

"We can tell them there's a fire on the floor above and get them out."

"What are we going to use for an explosive?"

"Let's hit the maintenance room. There have to be loads of chemicals we can use. We'll just grab a bunch, douse the room and the whole floor, light a match and run like hell."

Micah furrowed her brow. "Are you crazy? We're gonna blow ourselves up along with the building."

"This is the best we got," said Gideon. "We don't need all of us to do this. Two of us will light the chemicals while the others exit." Gideon grabbed Simon's arm. "Are you up for it?"

"Definitely."

"It was my idea to shut the portal; I'll take care of it." I couldn't bear the guilt if he died.

"Jess. Let me have this. I'll come back ... I promise."

I knew that in his mind, he needed to do this. He was up for the challenge. That's who he was. That's who I loved. I also knew if I didn't say what I truly felt, I would never be able to forgive myself.

"Gideon, I love you. I've always loved you, and I will never stop." I reached up to his lips and gently caressed them with mine.

He took me in his arms and held me close, his lips firmly pressing to mine. My heart raced as flutters of yearning replaced the aloof exterior I had tried so hard to maintain. The heat draped over me as I completely let go and melted into him. All the pain of the past few months faded away, and all that was left was him and me. He pulled away and nestled his cheek against my neck. I felt his hand softly trail through my hair. The only thing I could think of was a plea to the universe, please don't let him die.

I closed my eyes, letting his scent linger over me. When I opened them, Micah and Simon waited for us by the elevators.

It was time to get to work.

After a quick discussion, we agreed to look for the maintenance room on the hotel side. I remembered seeing some of the housekeeping personnel exit through a far door. We got a glimpse of one of the maids leaving. She held a caddy stocked with cleaning fluids. Thank the gods, it was exactly the room we needed.

Gathering off to the side of the check-in desk, we engaged in meaningless conversation so we wouldn't draw attention. Just three hotel guests discussing their itinerary for the day. When the moment felt right, we entered.

I scanned the front labels. "What should we use? Bleach? Drain cleaner? Ammonia?"

"Grab all of them," said Gideon.

We loaded up three buckets of industrial cleaning fluids and slipped out unnoticed.

I couldn't believe how smoothly it had gone. I was almost afraid to feel relieved.

I pressed the elevator button, and we stayed close together to hide the three buckets. My mouth felt dryer than the Mohave desert, and the back of my neck ached. The ding of our arriving car startled me, and the ache turned into a stabbing pain.

As the doors closed, I looked up at the floors. Four, five, six—we were there. We glanced out and down the hallway before hastily making our way to 629. My heart stopped when a guest three doors down exited his room, but he was too preoccupied looking down at his phone to notice us.

I inserted the key card and swiftly removed it. The latch clicked, and we piled in. I walked over to the window. The view that had started this crap was right in front of me—the neighborhood. It was so clear, and then in a moment, it was gone. Soon, it would be gone for good. I turned away. I didn't want to see that view anymore.

I sat on the bed beside Micah. Gideon and Simon lined up the bottles of destruction along the opposite side of the room.

I looked up at Gideon, and he pulled me up, grabbed my hand, and kissed it. I hugged his waist and rested my head on his chest ... so much time wasted on things that were not important. When we got home, I just wanted to hug everyone I love and keep them close. I'd tell them every day how much they mean to me and never forget how quickly things can change.

Simon gazed out of the window. "Blimey, we could use some of that."

"What?" I asked, clamoring to the window.

"See that white truck down there." He pointed. "It's the groundskeeper. I saw him here last week when Catherine and I first arrived. I bet he's got fertilizer."

"Let's get some," I said. "Gideon, do you wanna go with me."

Gideon backhanded Simon's upper arm. "Hold down the fort. We'll be back."

"Jess ..." Micah hugged me. "Don't die."

"Wasn't planning on it."

CHAPTER 14
KABOOM

WE WALKED THROUGH THE CASINO, weaving through the cluster of slot machines for camouflage, as we ambled to the main entrance. Breezing by the weekend gamblers, I checked each face for Smith or any of the grey goons. I knew that many of the casino and hotel employees were aliens, but none of them looked our way. Not that it did anything to shake the feeling that all eyes were on us. Distracted by an elderly woman hobbling with a walker, I didn't notice Gideon's abrupt stop and plowed right into him. Standing under the bright lights of the casino entrance were Smith and four of the grey goons.

We slipped behind one of the Wheel of Fortune slot machines and peeked out as the five figures casually entered the casino. Tourists are oblivious when gambling, so the four oversized men didn't draw a single look. We stuck together like glue, using the aisle that separated the machines from the poker tables. My pulse raced, and the weight on my chest alerted me I was on the way to another panic attack if I didn't slow things down. Taking three deep breaths, I concentrated on my last birthday. My mom had gotten Micah and me a gift card to a new spa that had opened. We had the best day. As the heaviness lifted, my body relaxed, and I was able to gain control. I won't say calm came over me, more like a sliver of reassurance that we could do this.

We kept our eyes on them as they made their way to the cafe and disappeared.

Blending in with the newly arrived guests and their luggage, we slipped out of the casino and approached the truck. Taking lookout, I pivoted and saw three landscapers in the distance, blowing off the sidewalk and clipping some of the plants, but the truck was unattended.

Gideon peered inside. "Yes!"

"Thank the gods," I murmured.

Gideon leaned over the side and grabbed a bag. It was heavier than he had anticipated, and he had to stand on the tire to gain leverage. Once he maneuvered it out, however, he could carry it. It was a bit awkward, but he managed to shift it in his arms, and we headed back to the casino.

"This bag is gonna stick out like a sore thumb," he grunted.

"We got no other choice. Let's keep our heads down and move."

We rummaged through the sea of lost dreams to the elevator, but this time eyes were on us. A tall, voluptuous woman stood at the bar, her curve-hugging black dress partially hidden under her long, blonde tresses. The chill of her steel blue eyes locked onto our every move.

As the doors shut, we saw Smith and the aliens pouring out from the cafe.

I gripped the rail that protruded from the wall of our elevator car. For each floor that passed, I tightened my finger grip. Six floors could have easily been twenty-six as the walls began to close in. *No, no, no. Not now.* Luckily, my focus toggled from me to Gideon, quieting the uprising in my body. The weight of the bag was becoming unmanageable as Gideon crouched over and slipped his right hand underneath the bag, hoisting it up with his knee. I grabbed one end and jiggled it to level it out.

A slight jolt followed by the doors welcoming us to the sixth floor brought a cool blast to the hair matted alongside my forehead. Hobbling to the room, the bag slipping through my fingers, my eyes scanned the open hallway for any unwanted interruptions. Thankfully, it was all clear, and we reached our destination without an issue.

I pounded the door with my foot. Simon unlocked it, and we stepped in, dropping the bag on the floor.

"Smith and the grey goons are here," I gasped. "They're downstairs in the casino, but they're going to be heading up in the very near future. We need to do this now."

Simon knelt, reading the front of the bag. "While you were gone, I checked a few recipes online. If we mix this with the other chemicals, we should have the kind of blowout we need to really destroy this place."

"Once we start this, we're gonna have to move quickly." Gideon began twisting caps off the chemical bottles. "Simon and I will set up the room while the rest of you get everyone off the floors. Then we'll cover the hallway with some of it, too. We need to do this right the first time because I don't think we're getting any second chances."

As the guys tossed the fertilizer around the room, I grabbed my bag and headed for the door. Gideon stopped me and took the bag. "No, babe, leave everything. We don't want to be slowed down by bags or anything else. Only us." I put my hand to his cheek and then dropped the bag on the floor. Gideon leaned in, gently kissing my lips. "I love you," I mouthed.

"I love you, too, baby."

The two of us divided the floors so we could get to everyone as quickly as possible. Micah ran down to the fifth, and I stayed on the sixth. We had just enough time to empty both floors—we prayed that it would be enough.

Gideon set a small fire in the trash can just inside our room. The smoke would billow out into the hallway and hopefully scare everyone so they would exit.

Furiously I banged on each door, screaming, "Fire!" At first, it was as if no one heard or even cared. But when Gideon held the smoke-filled can up to a smoke detector in the hallway, people started pouring out of their rooms. I directed them to the staircase, shouting. The bigger commotion, the better—we didn't want anyone left behind.

A couple with three small children rushed from a room two doors down from ours. They noticed the smoke, and their faces twisted with fear. I hated frightening them, but it was the only way to ensure their safety. I motioned for them to go down the stairs. I figured the staircase was what the fire department always advised us to use when we had our assemblies in high school. Every year they'd come out and demonstrate fire safety, and it had stuck with me. Besides, it would buy us a bit more time with Smith. Guests didn't use the stairs often, so it might take a little longer to notice them evacuating.

Micah got back within minutes. Apparently, most of the guests on the fifth floor were in town for a poker tournament and had already gone to the casino—a lucky break for us.

"Let's divide the hallway. I'll continue on the left, and you take the right."

"Gotcha." Micah agreed.

I had ushered out most of my side when I caught a glimpse of Micah out of the corner of my eye; she was having trouble with two guests. They were an elderly couple, and the man was in a wheelchair. She tried to assist them by pushing him, but his wife kept returning to the room for personal belongings. Micah had the wheelchair in one hand and the woman's arm in the other, but she was losing the battle. The woman broke free and wandered back into the room. I finished up with the last two rooms and ran down to help her.

She threw her arms in the air as she saw me approach. "Hey, she won't listen. His wife, she went back inside."

"Get him to the elevator. I'll get her even if I have to carry her out." I found the woman sitting on the bed, furiously rummaging through a large black leather satchel. It reminded me of the bag Mary Poppins carried, except instead of a lamp, she pulled out jewelry and laid it neatly on the bed: a row of chains, arranged from longest to shortest, and then bracelets, each one more intricate than the last. Pearls, diamonds, rubies —this woman had more precious stones than Tiffany's.

"Ma'am, we have to leave now. There's a fire, and your husband is waiting for you at the elevator. We need to get downstairs." I waited for a response, but nothing. She just kept at the task at hand. I inched closer to her and peered into the bag. She'd rolled up individual pieces of felt fabric, each one presumably containing a piece of jewelry. Gently, she'd place one on the bed and carefully unroll the fabric. Again, I urged her to get up, but still silence. And then—

"I know you're lying." Her tone was lilting, almost comforting.

"Excuse me?" I was flabbergasted.

"My dear, I know who you and your friends are. We have been on your planet for a long time. I was a young girl just like you when I first came here. So many changes for your people. It all happened too quickly."

I nervously tapped my foot on the floor. "Ma'am, we really have to go."

"I'm just so happy that it's finally over. My Timothy and I can go home. My only sadness is that we've aged so terribly while we were here. I don't know how your people do it. It's over so abruptly for you. But we will get to see our family and friends again, so I don't mind too much. We did like it here. You are a very interesting species."

"You're one of them?"

"Isn't that what I just told you, dear? Is there something wrong with your hearing? On my planet, I'm sure we could probably help you. Correcting things like vision and hearing is simple, no matter the issue."

"But saving your people from extinction—that escapes you?"

"Well, it is a bit more complicated than that, isn't it?"

"So, what are you doing here with this jewelry?" I tried to move the conversation along.

"I was trying to find a very special bracelet. My husband gave it to me when we first married. I'd like to bring it back with me. Oh, here it is."

I looked at the bracelet she had clutched in her hand in surprise. It had no diamonds or any other stones. It was a simple thin gold chain with a dangling small solid heart. The heart had something written across it, but I was too far away to read it.

"Why this one in particular?" Curiosity had definitely gotten the best of me. "What's written on it?"

"We were not married on our planet. We came here together and fell in love while serving our people. On the day of our union, he spotted this in a small jewelry store. We were in downtown Las Vegas. In those days, it was the popular place to be. He walked to meet me at one of the chapels when he bought it. It was the first thing from this planet that he had given me. For me, it represents all the work we tried to do here. We have given our hearts and our lives for our planet. Fortunately, we found each other in the process. Now that the time has come to go home, I would like this one reminder of the years we spent here together. We came simply, our hearts still open to hope. That is what is written on the charm—hope."

"Hope is good to have."

"Both of us have grown to love you and your planet. We miss ours, yes. And we are eager to get there again. But it could have been a far worse place that they sent us to. Yes, we definitely feel a bit of sadness leaving here."

I sat, no words coming to me—all this time running from Smith and the grey goons. To me, they were all nothing more than monsters: a heartless, ice-veined species of maniacal deviants who would annihilate us to save themselves, with no thought or conscience about what they had to do. But this woman expressed genuine sadness. The thought of giving up all those loved ones for such a long time melted my heart. I couldn't do it. I wouldn't do it.

"What is your name and your husband's?"

"Why, dear? Why would that have any meaning to you?"

"Please. I want to know."

"I go by Marion, and my husband is Timothy. We took those names when we came here. I think our given names would strike you as odd. Now tell me, why is knowing our names so important to you?"

"It makes you real. Unlike Smith and the thugs he hangs with, you and your husband are real people, like me and my friends. And for some reason, that gives *me* hope." I softened. "Would you like me to put it on for you?"

She looked up at me, the bracelet clutched in her shaking hand. She nodded.

I fastened the bracelet around her left wrist and put my arm out for her to hold. We traipsed down the hallway to the elevator, where Micah waited with Timothy.

I made a mental agreement to myself not to let Micah know who they were. There was plenty of time for that later, once all of this was over.

I pushed the button, and the grinding of metal came from above right before the doors parted. Micah wheeled Timothy into the car, and I guided Marion in beside him. As the doors closed, she grabbed the charm dangling on her bracelet. I knew I had just met her and would most likely never see either of them again, but that didn't ease the hollowness in my chest. She had, in this brief moment, made her people *human* to me. Smith was a muted version, and the grey goons were his soldiers, but people like Timothy and Marion were the life that made the planet turn. They put in the true sacrifice, and they were the ones who had paid the highest price.

I must have gotten lost in my thoughts because the next thing I knew, Micah grabbed my hand and yanked. She wanted to be certain that everyone had left, so we did a fast door-to-door, rapping with our fists as we ran by and then headed back to 629.

The guys had torn the drapes from the windows, rolled them up, and placed them on the floor. They stretched from the room all the way out of the door and midway down the hallway. I nestled up to Gideon and planted one last kiss on his full lips.

"Hey, we're all clear. What are you guys doing?" I placed my hand over his heart.

"Setting the drapes up to be a fuse. They're fire-retardant, so they'll burn slower. This will give us time to get the hell away from here before the real explosion hits."

"Almost done here; you two should head out. Me and Gideon will light the drapes and then haul arse down the stairs. We'll meet up in the parking garage near your car.

It was a logical plan. Now it just had to work.

Pounding down the stairs to the lobby, my hand glided over the rail, barely making contact. I wasn't sure if anyone could hear the echoes of rubber soles as they hammered the gaudy, gold marble, but to me, it sounded like a warning beacon to the searching Smith.

When we reached the lobby, I held my breath. The alien hit squad could be waiting for us. As the doors opened, I half-closed my eyes, but there was no one there.

We passed a big commotion in the middle of the hotel lobby; a mob of guests was frantically informing the staff about the fire. I saw a large man in a dark suit—a grey goon. He glanced toward the center of the casino, and I followed his line of sight. *Smith.* I tapped Micah and pointed, and then Smith saw us. We bolted for the front of the room with both Smith and the grey goons closing in on either side of us.

"Split up! You know where to meet."

Maybe this diversion would help keep them off balance. I wasn't sure, but what I did know was that as long as they were chasing us, they didn't know about Gideon and Simon upstairs.

Micah charged the doors, and I darted left, running through the cafe and then the race and sportsbook. The three grey goons were right behind me, but Smith was nowhere in sight. I assumed he went after Micah.

I spotted an exit and charged through the doors and into the side parking lot. The garage was on the other end of the building.

As I weaved through the parked cars, I saw Micah aiming for the garage. Then, BOOM!

The explosion was loud enough to stop us and our pursuers in our tracks. I clapped my hands over my ears right before there was another loud blast. I turned my head, and a small flash in the desert caught my eye. The silhouette of a female straining to navigate her wheelchair-bound companion through the uneven terrain tugged at my heart. Marion and Timothy hadn't made it in time. The portal was destroyed, and they were stuck here.

I turned back to my current predicament just as Smith tightened the gap between him and Micah, two grey goons followed them. I glanced toward the desert one last time, expecting to see Marion and Timothy come back, but they didn't. They just kept going.

Smoke streamed out of the hotel windows, and crowds of guests were gathering outside the property. Some were screaming, and others ran in a panic to their cars, creating chaos.

I was dumbfounded watching a small tan Honda and black Nissan fight for the valet exit. Neither one wanted to concede, creating total obstruction to the cars behind them.

The staff tried keeping everyone together and calming them down, but their attempts were futile. Shouts of terrorism fueled the fear of the weary crowd, leaving a lullaby of screams and wailing.

I scanned the scores of frightened guests, hoping to spot Simon and Gideon, but they were nowhere in sight. I prayed they had exited out the back and were already on their way to the parking structure.

Someone shouted my name—bartender dude? "Don't go back to the casino; Smith left guards inside."

No worries there. "Why should you care?"

"I don't agree with any of this; I just want to go home."

"Be my guest."

"I'm sorry."

The dude took off running into the desert. Poor bastard, he doesn't realize the portals closed.

On my way to the garage, the grey goons resumed their pursuit. The drive to get to our destination became more intense. Every scenario possible was playing itself in my head.

As I turned the corner into the concrete and steel structure, I ran up the ramp to the second level. So wrapped up in what *could* happen, I didn't notice what was right in front of me. I bumped full speed into Gideon. I bounced off him like a pinball and landed on my ass. He reached his hand out, and I grabbed it. I wanted to slap him for making me worry about him, but instead, I put my arms around him and held him tightly. I could slap him later.

When we reached the top of the incline, Micah and Simon were waiting by my car. We waved and shouted, but they didn't respond. It wasn't until we were closer that we understood their lack of enthusiasm. Waiting behind them like judge, jury, and executioner, was Smith and the five grey goons.

Instinct kicked in, and we broke off like pieces of a puzzle. I went full steam to the right and up the incline, pumping to get to the next level. Micah and Simon barely escaped the grey goon's lunge. Micah caught up with me, and Simon bolted for the staircase. Gideon ran in the direction of the casino entrance. I couldn't help but feel like rats in a maze frantically hunting the cheese. Only our cheese was two compact cars equipped with air-conditioning and a straight shot to Vegas.

The grey goons split up, too, following everyone but Gideon. Before I reached the top of the next level, I saw Smith floating toward him, and he was advancing way too quickly. They both disappeared through the casino entrance just as we rounded the next level.

I had no idea what Smith was capable of but could easily imagine. We'd destroyed his portal, trapping him in our world. The vengeance he might bring was terrifying.

As Micah and I zigzagged through the cars to evade our would-be captors, I spotted Simon leaping from the staircase. Three grey goons were on his heels, and he shouted for us to keep going. We heeded his advice, ricocheting between parked cars, trying to confuse the two aliens behind us. We shot ahead of them and ran to level three, ducking behind a row of oversized SUVs.

As I crouched next to Micah, my stomach roiled, the heat growing with each passing minute.

The two grey goons were still searching for us as Simon came charging up the stairs, steamrolling to the next level. A few moments later, the other three goons tumbled from the staircase, gasping for breath.

I leaned into Micah and, in a muffled voice, said, "If we could completely wear those guys out, we might have a good chance of escaping."

"Any ideas?"

"Let's go up to the next level using the ramp. It's pretty damn steep; I think it'll be a lot harder for them than using the stairs. It just may do them in." I silently made a plea to the universe that this idea had substance.

We jumped out from behind the cars and shouted to draw their attention before scrambling up the incline. I glanced over my shoulder; the two grey goons were stumbling on their feet and getting slower and slower with each unsteady step. By the time we reached the top, they had been reduced to a crawl.

Planted at the rim of level four, we peered down at our plan in motion. On the ground, practically at our feet, were the three grey goons who'd been pursuing Simon. They could barely catch their breath.

He saw us and hastened over. I scoured the area to find out where our two alien trackers were at this point. They had collapsed about three-quarters of the way up the incline. I wasn't sure if it was their size, or that they were slow to begin with, or maybe our gravity was a bit different and affected them more. Whatever the reason, it was working to our advantage.

"We need something to restrain these wankers," said Simon. "Once we have them out of commission, we can concentrate on Smith. He's gonna be a little harder to stop." I tested the handles on nearby cars, searching for something to tie them up with. All I could think about was Gideon. Smith wouldn't tire like the grey goons. *Where the hell were they?*

"Hey, there was an electrical truck on level two," Micah whispered. "Maybe we can find something useful."

"Good idea, let's check it out."

On the way down, we passed the two collapsed goons who'd been pursuing us. I looked one of them right in the eyes. They twitched. Maybe the reality of being stuck here was starting to set in. I didn't know why, but I felt sorry for him. I remember what I felt when I was stuck on his planet: complete panic and despair. But then I quickly reminded myself that this was one of the beings who, minutes ago, was chasing us down to force us to do something I didn't even want to envision. Any empathy I might have felt just dissipated into *my* earth's air. On level two, we spotted the truck with *Jameson Electrical* on its side. In the bed of the truck was a large spool of electrical wire. It wasn't rope, but it just might work. Together Micah and I managed to hoist it over the side and maneuver it to the elevator. There was no way we were getting it up the ramp.

Simon gave us a thumbs up when we stepped from the doors rolling the latest fashion in alien bondage.

Grinning, Micah produced a pair of wire cutters she'd found in a toolbox in the truck.

We tied each grey goon's hands behind him and then bound their feet. They were too heavy to really move, so we improvised. It was actually sort of funny to roll these big bulky guys across the asphalt like donuts.

"Please, let us leave, and we won't bother you any longer. We don't have much time." One of them struggled to talk between rolls.

"We should have gagged them—wait, what did you say?" I grabbed Simon's arm, and we all stopped.

"You don't have much time for what?" I didn't like where this was going.

Simon stood between me and the grey goon who tried to wiggle out of his restraint. "Jessie, don't engage with him. He'll say whatever to get free."

"No. Please, I mean what I said. We will leave you alone. All we want now is to get home." Fear laced his voice. He pleaded.

"I'm sorry to break it to you, buddy, but you can't go back. We blew up the hotel room. Your beacon is gone, and the portal is closed. Smith said it takes a really long time to construct, so I think you're stuck here for the duration."

"No, we're not. The portal isn't shut yet. The frequency has a sixty-minute delay. We can still make it."

I thought back to Marion and Timothy. They weren't going back in vain—they knew there was a delay. It felt good to know they had made it home to Kamaria. Maybe the rest of the aliens from the casino and the hotel had, too. I looked at my watch. It had been twenty minutes since the explosion. In their weakened state, they would need every one of those remaining forty minutes to get back in time.

"Let them go."

"What? Have you lost your mind? No. We are not letting them go." Simon objected.

"Listen, I know you hate every one of them for what they did to Catherine. But it doesn't do us any good to keep them here. Their species is dying. By the time they get the portal back in operation, it will probably be too late. Let them go and be with the ones they love. Don't do to them what was done to you. Smith is a monster—yes. He sanctioned all of this. But the aliens on the ground are just soldiers carrying out orders, thinking they're doing what's right to save their people. If we let them go now, they'll barely have time to make it, but we need to let them try."

I turned. "Micah? What do you think?"

Micah gently touched Simon's shoulder. "Please don't be angry with me for what I'm about to say, but I agree. It's like any war: the real criminals are never the ones fighting the battle. They're just doing what they were told. Thinking it's the right thing to do." Her voice was so soft, I could barely hear her, but I know Simon caught every word. His face relaxed, and his shoulders slumped.

"I won't lie. I don't trust them. This could all be a trick, but I don't think it is. They're all so weak right now. If we untied them and it was a lie, I doubt they'd have the energy to harm us."

"Okay, mates. You've all made your point. We'll let the blokes go."

Micah and I untied them one by one while Simon waited, wire wrapped around his closed fist and ready for battle. But once freed, all five of them wearily stumbled out of the parking garage and scattered toward the desert. We watched until we could no longer see them and then went back to the casino to look for Gideon.

TWO POLICE VEHICLES, a fire truck, and an ambulance sat parked at the curb. We snuck into the casino through the entrance near the quarter poker machines. Normally this area would be filled with people hoping to win a royal flush and make their way home a thousand dollars richer. But today, it was empty. The further into the building we went, the more we realized how many people had been aliens. I looked out of the glass front doors into the lobby and saw a few patrons talking with the emergency team, but there weren't many.

"I'll be back in a sec. I wanna see if someone outside saw anything ... like a floating guy." I had the glass doors in my sights.

Micah chimed in, "Great idea, I'll go with you."

"Sounds good mates, while you two are out there, I think I'll start looking for Gideon on the first floor."

We'll meet you at the staircase in 10 minutes."

"Works for me," said Simon.

Outside, the officers were questioning the remaining guests and employees. Micah and I listened while they told stories about most of the staff and some of the guests walking out into the desert. They concluded that these people must have been in shock because when urged to stop, they just kept going.

The ambulance prepared to leave as there weren't any injuries more serious than a few bumps and scrapes.

"I wonder how come we don't see any firefighters in the casino?"

"They're probably on the sixth floor, making sure the fire is out. You know how these things can simmer," suggested Micah.

I nodded my head in agreement; after all the weirdness of the past few days, what was once odd had become matter of fact. Maybe they were on the sixth floor—maybe not. At this point, it wasn't my main concern. Gideon was.

A man lingered by the remaining first response vehicles. He was about sixty, and his thick, white, wavy hair framed a well-chiseled chin and smooth complexion. His tall, thin frame drenched in a tailored dark grey suit could've been this month's cover of GQ. Aside from the nervous pacing, his expression was cool and confident.

"Excuse me, sir, could we talk to you for a moment?" When he turned and faced me, he looked a little familiar. I couldn't place where I might have seen him—maybe in the bar or the mall before all of this started.

"Well, it is my experience that when not one but two beautiful women ask to speak with you, you give them your undivided attention." Hmm—a charmer. *Where have I seen him before?*

"Thank you. We were wondering if you might have seen anything—uh, unusual?"

"You mean more unusual than the entire floor of the hotel blowing up or half the casino and hotel population walking off into the empty desert? Strange like that?" *Sarcasm. I didn't see that coming.*

"Actually, yes."

"Well, Jessie, then I'd have to say no."

I froze. How the hell did he know my name? Had Micah realized what had just happened? I glanced at her; a patch of asphalt burn on her arm preoccupied her. Nope.

He checked his watch.

"Need to be somewhere?" I tried to be coy.

"Something like that."

"How do you know me?"

"Well, you and your friend just came over to talk to me."

"No. You called me Jessie." That got Micah's attention. "I never told you my name." The hairs on my arms stood at attention. Micah grabbed my hand and slowly backed up, but I wasn't going anywhere. Sure, I was scared, but I was so tired of all this crap. "Tell me how you know me."

And then it clicked. The man had kept eyeing his watch—he was one of *them*. "You're waiting for Jonathon Smith, aren't you? You're from the other world."

"Yes, Jessie. Right on both accounts. Beautiful and smart—a lethal combination, my dear girl. I will not harm you. Don't be afraid."

"You know what, mister, I am so beyond afraid. I'm tired and completely over your people. Why are you still here anyway? Smith probably wouldn't wait for you, and the portal is closing in less than twenty-five minutes."

"I doubt that."

"No, I'm pretty sure because we blew up room 629. Your ticket home is about to expire, buddy, so I suggest you start making a shot for the desert."

"Has anyone ever told you that you speak most eloquently?" *Huh, there's that sarcasm again.*

"What I was referring to was the fact that I doubted he would leave me behind."

"Well, then you don't know Jonathon Smith very well, do you?"

"Actually, I know him quite well. He's my brother." Damn, I knew he looked familiar. He resembled Smith but with more refined and handsome features.

Micah yanked on my arm so hard it nearly came out of the socket. "Ouch!"

"Sorry, but we have to go now."

"I told you both, I won't harm you. I am merely waiting for my brother."

"Your brother is busy chasing down our friends inside the casino."

"Then I must go in and retrieve him. There is no time for this."

"I'm guessing you're the one with the brains."

"Ah, I see you have a bit of sarcasm yourself."

Once again, I found myself at a loss for words. *What made him say that?? Could he read my mind? Was he doing it now?*

"The answer to your questions, my dear girl, is yes, yes, and yes."

"Yes, what?"

"Yes, I can read your mind."

"Okay, that's just creepy, Mr."

"Wilhelm Smith."

"Huh?"

"My name is not Mister. It is Wilhelm Smith."

"Twenty-two minutes and counting, Wilhelm."

"Ladies, I suggest we go inside and get your friends and my brother so that we may leave while there's still time."

Micah and I walked a few feet behind our new acquaintance. No way were we trusting a mind-reading douche bag to be at our backs. Something had been gnawing at me since we were guests on Kamaria, and my total frustration overrode any sense of caution.

"Hey, Wilhelm. Answer this, buddy; how come you,

Smith, the goons, and the resident aliens at Primm could see us? When we were on your twisted version of a planet, none of your people could."

"It's a small device implanted behind the eyes. It allows us to view color the same way as humans do. Anyone involved in the mission is equipped with the device."

"Great. You can figure out how to see the colors of the rainbow but not how to save your people. Your science is kind of shitty."

"Why? Have your people cured cancer? Famine? Changed the tides of global warming? There's a saying people use on this planet that I've always found profound. People in glass houses shouldn't throw stones."

I tried to think of a brick wall. I didn't want the hot alien knowing I agreed.

"Too late." Wilhelm smirked.

"Dude, that's wrong on so many levels."

Once in the casino, we went directly to the staircase where Simon waited. When he saw Wilhelm, Simon fisted both hands. We spoke quickly and managed to calm him down, explaining who he was and that he only wanted to get Smith and leave.

I left out the part about the mind-reading, figuring it might freak him out too much. Wilhelm silently agreed with me. Apparently, he could telepathically answer you, too—double creepy. We were taking a risk in trusting Wilhelm, but we did share one goal—to find Smith. So, we worked together. Micah, Simon, and I took the second floor, and Wilhelm took the third. Emergency crews had shut off the power, and it was rough searching in the dim glow from the backup generator.

Halfway down the hall, Smith came floating around the corner.

"Smith! We've met your brother. Living in your brothers' shadow, are you? He's good-looking and charming, obviously none of the qualities you inherited." I taunted him some more. "He's looking for you, and he's not happy. It kind of felt like he disagrees with what you've been doing here."

"My brother is not my keeper."

He waved his hand, sending all three of us catapulting down the hall and slamming hard into the wall.

I'm really getting tired of this shit.

Gideon must have heard our screaming because he ran from one of the rooms armed with a chair—apparently his new weapon of choice, although it didn't do him much good on Kamaria.

Smith was focused on Simon, Micah, and I and didn't notice Gideon come up behind him until the chair hit the back of his legs. The floating fiend toppled to the floor like a shaky game of Jenga.

I sprang to my feet, grabbed a handful of Micah's T-shirt, and yanked her up. The three of us joined Gideon in a full-out sprint, rapidly filling him in on what happened as we flew up the stairs, shouting for Wilhelm.

There was no answer. We were in the hallway between the elevator and the set of rooms when we heard a loud crack. I looked back, and there was Smith. He had blasted open the staircase door with such force that it embedded into the wall.

My first reaction was to scream, but I stopped myself. He hadn't seen us yet, so we slipped into one of the rooms and hid.

Doors burst open one by one as he made his way down the hallway. The screeching of nails digging into the wall took my breath away. My heart hammered against my chest while we scrambled to find a place to hide.

I scampered under the bed, and Micah and Simon tucked away in the luggage closet. Gideon slid behind the heavy dark draperies that flanked the front window. My eyes grew wide as the door flung open. Bam! The force knocked the top portion of the door off its hinges.

Smith's heavy breathing filled the room. I shuddered each time he passed me. When his feet floated toward the door, I quietly celebrated.

I was getting ready to slide out when all hell broke loose.

The bed next to mine was jerked off the floor and thrown across the room, hitting the window and the curtains. Gideon slithered to the floor, his head bleeding. Micah and Simon scrambled from the closet, tumbling over each other to the floor. Micah let out a spine-tingling scream and passed out when she saw Gideon lying in a pool of his own blood.

Smith spun around, his face ruby red. He began to raise his hand again, then suddenly stopped. I scrambled to my feet and picked up the flat screen, hurling it at our pissed-off alien. It stopped dead in midair and then redirected toward Simon. It slammed into him with such force that it threw him back into the bathroom and against the mirror, shattering it.

I scrambled to my feet, trying to reach Gideon, but Smith caught me in a choke hold. I struggled to escape but only managed to twist far enough to see the bloody mess that was Gideon's head and chest.

"Since I couldn't grab you both, one will have to be enough," he hissed.

"Where the hell are you taking me? Look, you moron, you only have about fifteen minutes to get back. The portal is about to close. Your brother is looking for you, although I have no idea why, and you're going to miss your chance to get home."

"No, I won't. I'm going there right now. What Wilhelm does is up to him."

"I told him."

"You told him what?"

"That if the situation were reversed, you wouldn't go back to help him."

"You don't understand. This is beyond family. Beyond a brother's tie. Our entire species depends on the success of our experiments. I can't take the time to find him and lose access to our planet. What's at stake is far too vast for one brother."

"Really, brother? You would leave me here stuck on this planet for the rest of my years? For what? To try and fail yet again? We have been at this for centuries and to no avail. Maybe our people are not meant to go on. Maybe it is time we just enjoy what we have, the time we are given." I hadn't seen Wilhelm come in, Smith looked frustrated, and I think Wilhelm knew.

"Yes, I do realize that, Jessie." Wilhelm spoke as if listening to someone's thoughts were common.

"Damn it. Stop that." I felt violated. Those were my thoughts.

"Are you reading minds again, brother?" Smith smirked.

"Well, Jonathon, they are so easy. It's like reading a child's book when I gain access to their thoughts. They put up no struggle at all." Wilhelm grinned at his brother.

"I'm so glad we can amuse you, Wilhelm." Now all I felt was anger.

"That one you're holding, brother—she's feisty. Packs a mean wit. I like her. But we cannot bring her back with us."

"Why not?" Smith sounded disappointed.

"Because she serves no purpose. She will not get us any closer to the solution. Both you and I know this. Besides, isn't it time all of this ends? Let her go, and let us get back to our planet before it is too late."

"I cannot. I will not. I am going back, but I am taking her with me."

"I won't let you do that. Please do not force me to fight you."

"Your choice, brother—but you have to catch up with me first."

Smith glided at record speed, whisking me through the near desolate casino. The few stragglers that were there wouldn't make eye contact with me as we weaved in and out of the quarter slots and down the center of the poker tables. I reached out, trying to grab a chair or the end of one of the tables, but Smith was calculating and yanked back. I struggled to get free, but the harder I fought, the stronger Smith's grip became. As I looked back at the growing distance between me and my friends, I couldn't help feeling like I would never see them again.

CHAPTER 16

IT'S OVER

A DEEP DENIM invaded upon the sky, stealing away the last of the persimmon rays glowing behind the faraway mountains. Blinking white, yellow, and amber bulbs of the casinos in the distance cast the only light by which I could make out my surroundings. My legs, dangling like noodles, tingled and grew numb. The sand blowing in Smith's self-made gust cut like glass across my cheeks. I shut my eyes. *No sense going blind even if I was gonna be a baby factory on an alien planet.*

The last thing I saw was a cloud of dust hanging far in the distance behind us. It could only be Wilhelm. He glided so fast it was like he had a jet engine strapped to his back.

The stinging subsided, and I realized Smith had slowed down. Peeling my lids back slowly, it took a second for my eyes to focus on the row of houses. He released his grip, and I slithered to the ground. I briskly rubbed my legs to regain circulation.

Peering up at Smith, I let the words fly. "Listen, you gliding piece of crap, let me go. I promise if you take me back to Kamaria, I will do everything I can to make your life a living hell." I was scared, but I wasn't going to let him know that.

"I think you have that backward. It will be you who will suffer for the trouble you and your friends have caused me and my people. I will take no precautions or make any attempt to make our experiments easier on you. You, girl, will get the full brunt of what we have to do. You may have cost my people their very existence, and you will pay a high price for that."

"Brother, this isn't the way. Our people would not want this." Wilhelm shouted.

I leaned to see past Smith. His brother had caught up with us. Under the twinkle of the big dipper, Wilhelm's chiseled features were even more handsome than they were from the illumination of the casino lights.

"They don't want it. I have heard many disturbing stories over the past decade from those who have been posted here with you. I chose not to believe them. I thought they were just yearning to come home and had greatly exaggerated. But I can see now I was an ignorant fool. The stories are true. I've witnessed some of them with my own eyes. I would have never believed you were capable of such atrocities. The things you've done went far beyond what our intentions were."

Smith looked away. "We were getting nowhere. I did what had to be done. What no one else had the strength to do." He grabbed my arm and squeezed, cutting off the blood flow. I tried to pull away, but his grip was too strong.

"We are so close, Wilhelm. I know with just a little more time we would have gotten the information we needed to save our people. But this girl and her friends have ruined everything. And I will not allow it to have been for nothing. She is our last chance to find our cure, and I will make sure we take every liberty with her to do so. She will pay for interfering. I will exhaust her body to every extreme to save our people."

Sadness drew Wilhelm's face down. "I would not have believed any of this if I had not heard the poisonous words drip from your mouth. I will hold myself accountable for turning a blind eye and a deaf ear. But now I see and hear fully the evil you have allowed yourself to regress to. Brother—this will not save our people. We have been trying for so long. It is time to realize that we have lived out our existence. We still have a few generations left who can go on and maybe achieve what we set out to do. But for us, it is time to let go. Do not leave us a legacy tainted with such horrors that it blackens all the good. Do not undo us—our people."

"But we still have one more chance. She could be the one. She's strong—stronger than anyone else we brought back. This could be it. Are you willing to throw all of it away just for one girl?"

"Yes. I am. Because she is more than one girl. She represents the divide between our dark side and our light. We were always good, our people a peaceful race. Priding ourselves on the fact that we had evolved to a stage free of war, hatred, and destruction. But what you've done sets us back thousands of years. The end does not justify the means. Let her go. We only have a few minutes left to make it home. Don't waste our time here any longer."

The alien's conversation grew distant as the hum of a racing engine captured my ears. I put my hand in front of my eyes to block the blinding beam jettisoning from the dead of night. My pulse raced as the compact car emerged from the parched landscape of bottlebrush and tumbleweeds in a cloud of dust and debris. It skidded to an abrupt halt, and my friends piled out.

Micah and the guys lined up next to Wilhelm, and the car headlights illuminated their dried blood and punctured flesh. Their wide eyes and clenched jaws told me they were ready for battle.

Smith looked down at the ground as if he were broken and

could no longer speak. I felt his grip start to lessen, and slowly he released my arm. As I dropped down on my feet, he stopped me one last time.

Looking into my eyes, he said, "It's all an illusion."

It made no sense, but I didn't care. As far as I was concerned, Smith was well on his way to being completely loony. Whatever came out of his mouth was probably gibberish from those scrambled eggs he had as a brain. All I wanted was to get free and join Gideon and my friends. This crazy train was finally at its last stop, and I was getting off.

"Wilhelm?" Smith spoke softly.

"Yes?"

"Did everyone get back?"

"Yes, they did. Now it is time for us to go. Start ahead, brother. I'll catch up in a moment."

When Smith was a distance away, Wilhelm panned the four of us and took one last gaze into the desert. "You really do have a lovely planet. So majestic. I'm sorry for what my brother has done to you and your people. Simon, I cannot bring back your wife. I wish with all the stars in the universe that I could, but it is impossible.

"I hope that you can contrive some comfort in knowing that if it weren't for her, I would have never believed that Jonathon committed such horrible acts. You and yours are safe. We will not be back. They are good people from my world; please know this."

Simon looked away.

I don't think he really cared about anything Wilhelm had to say. But for some reason, I did. "I believe you."

"You do?"

"Yes. I don't think your people are bad. I talked with Marion for a bit back in the room. She and Timothy were just doing what they were told. They believed they were saving your planet. I don't even think they knew the extent of some of the experiments. I think Smith kept most of that to himself. I'm not sure, and it isn't really important anymore. The point is, I know. She was sweet. Devoted to her husband and her people. I don't think she was capable of directly harming anyone."

Micah raised a brow. "When did this all happen?"

"Back in the hotel room when you wheeled Timothy to the elevator. That's why she wouldn't come. She was looking for a bracelet he had gotten for her years ago. It had 'hope' written on a heart. She said that's what she had...hope. I felt her pain when she spoke to me. Practically their whole life was given up for what they thought was a good reason. All they wanted to do now was to get home to their friends and family and their world. So yes, Wilhelm, I know."

"That's why it took you so long." Micah gently smiled.

"Yeah."

Simon stepped forward and stood directly in front of Wilhelm. I had no idea what he was going to do; the buzzing in my ears grew louder. *Please, Simon, let it go.* His stance relaxed as he held his arm out for a shake. Wilhelm just looked at his extended hand in confusion.

I must admit, it was the first time I had chuckled in a while. I grabbed Wilhelm's arm and extended it. "Put your hand out and grasp his. It's a custom here. He's wishing you well and saying it's okay. It packs a lot of meaning for our people."

Wilhelm looked at me and then back at Simon. They shook hands.

"A strange custom but unexpectedly gratifying," said Wilhelm. "I wish all of you well and a long and happy life."

I had to ask. "What about your brother? What will happen to him?"

"I'm not sure yet. We have a council that handles affairs like this. I must say we haven't had to use them in a very long time. But we will meet, and it will be decided. Whatever our decision, it can't be as tormenting as living with your own memories. I feel my brother will be paying for his actions for the rest of his life."

"I'm sorry, but I can't say that I feel sorry for him." Everyone nodded.

"I understand. But now, time is fleeting, and I must go."

As he turned to leave, we could see Smith waiting in the distance by the portal house. He shouted something that I missed, but I could hear Wilhelm's answer. "No. I do not think that is a wise idea. It is best they find out for themselves."

We gaped at each other. What was he not telling us? "Tell us what?" Gideon and Simon asked in unison.

"Gentlemen, I really must go now."

"But wait ..."

Wilhelm didn't wait. In a millisecond, he floated away and was down at the other end of the block. He and Smith disappeared into the house, and then, seconds later, the entire neighborhood was gone. It took me a moment to realize that it was truly over.

We were free.

———

We crammed into the car and drove to the casino. My Altima sat waiting for us in the parking garage. Micah smiled and I handed her the keys. She and Simon hopped in and they followed behind Gideon and me. We all bid a middle finger to Primm and got on the highway toward Las Vegas and home.

It was dark, and the desert displayed a landscape of

silhouettes. As I reviewed the events of the past several days, I knew something for sure: we wouldn't be telling anyone. Journals or not, it no longer mattered. They were gone, and they weren't coming back—it was over. Nobody would know that the four of us actually helped save the human race, but it didn't matter. We could go back to our normal lives and boring routines, which sounded like Disneyland right about now.

I glanced in the side-view mirror at the lights from Primm fading behind us. They danced along the horizon, twinkling, as they reached for the heavens. I turned my head to view the shadow of mountains and then back to the lights, but they were gone. *Huh, they're out of sight? That was fast.*

"What do you suppose he meant?" Gideon asked.

"Who?"

"Wilhelm. When we were back in the desert. He shouted out to Smith that we didn't need to know just yet."

"Who knows? Smith was operating on sheer crazy. Maybe Wilhelm was just humoring him. He didn't seem like a bad guy. I mean, he sounded genuine. Don't you think?"

"Yes, he did. But I don't know, it's just nagging at me."

"It's over, and we're all okay. I'm so tired. All I want is my bed."

"You're right." Gideon half-smiled. "We made it."

I turned to him, but he was already staring.

"What? Watch the road."

His eyes traveled between me and the highway. There was a longing—something I had never seen before.

"I love you. You're my world. When we were chasing Smith after he had grabbed you, I felt like everything was lost. I can't imagine another day without you. I know I haven't been able to tell you that before, but I'm saying it—hell, I'm shouting it. I love you forever, Jessie Marshall. I want a life with you. I hope you want the same."

I reached my hand out, caressed the back of his neck, and then ran my fingers through his hair.

"I love you too."

He softly grinned, and he clasped my hand to his chest. I slid closer to him. It was all going to be okay.

Over the next forty-five minutes, I reflected on the mural of events that began with the drive from Las Vegas to Primm. It had been so uneventful. None of us could have imagined the journey we would endure. All I wanted was to see my mom and dad again.

The drive was blessedly quiet. Gideon didn't bother to put on the radio, and I didn't ask him to. I needed to think. The quiet gave me time to settle down. Life was going to be better now. I wondered if Micah would stay in touch with Simon. The man had just lost his wife, and he could use a friend who understood what he had gone through. We had control of our future, thanks to Wilhelm. I hoped that one day someone from their planet would find a cure, and their people could go on. I would probably never know, but we were home, and it was time to work on the things we could change. We were all going to be okay. We still had each other, our families, and our friends. And now, a greater appreciation for what that really means.

We drove past the two framing hills that signified we were about to enter "Oz," a term we coined for Las Vegas. When we reached the peak of the road, we could see the Valley. It was more beautiful to me than ever before, and the lights were a reminder that we were not alone.

I grabbed my phone out of my purse. I wanted to call my mom and let her know I was okay. It had been days since she heard from me, and I knew she had probably passed panic a long time ago. All our families had to be crazy by now.

I gazed at my messages. Why weren't there numerous voice mails of sheer terror from Mom? That was odd. As I searched for her name in my contacts list, I took one more glance at the warm and inviting lights of Las Vegas and then—darkness.

ACKNOWLEDGMENTS

To Bobbi Bush, thank you for always being by my side and for never quitting on me. I love you more than words could ever express, la mia bella Sorella.

To Stevie and Lee,
Thank you for every late night horror movie, years of laughter, hugs through the tears, and simply for being you.

Quote
The strength of a civilization is not measured by its ability to fight wars, but rather by its ability to prevent them. - Gene Roddenberry

ABOUT THE AUTHOR

Born Vicki-Ann Guidice, on January 14th, 1962, her journey into the realm of the spiritual and supernatural was initiated at birth. Her early years were spent in Queens, New York known for having more people passed on than alive, as well as having several Gothic cemeteries within walking distance of its communities. At the age of 15, she moved to Los Angeles California taking her fertile imagination with her. After meeting her future husband, Ronald Bush, her new homeland became Las Vegas, Nevada.

As a mother of two, her first published book in 2008, Winslow Willow the Woodland Fairy, took her love of fantasy and spun it into a heartwarming children's book. The progression to the young adult literary market took root in her novels that captured the haunting qualities of the Las Vegas desert surrounding her, but it was New York that called her home. Alex McKenna, the main character in the book series first published in 2019, is the embodiment of her Italian American roots, memories of adolescent outsider status, and the strength it takes to live an authentic life.

Ms. Bush is a co-founder of Coffee House Tours, an events-based collaboration between local bookstores and coffee shops allowing authors to represent themselves and their works. Additionally, she is a frequent podcast literary guest and has a special relationship with The Center LGBTQIA+ Las Vegas where Alex McKenna has been an inspirational focus as a transgender Paranormal teen. Now starring in the short film Alex and Margret's Beginning, inspired by the book series, Ms. Bush is an award-winning short screenplay writer and Producer. Bringing her moving and unique storyline and character to a broader audience.